TOIL AND TROUBLE

Kingdom of Summer Wood: Book One

Jaelyn Elliott

To those who find magic in falling leaves and the autumn breeze.

Chapter 1

Allie looked up from her homework at the tinkling of the shop bell. Pushing a strand of dark auburn hair behind her ear, she smiled at the couple entering. "Welcome to Silver Quill Gifts. Can I help you with anything?" she asked as she shoved her college textbook under the counter.

"Oh, no thank you, we're just looking for now."

"If you have any questions, let me know." Allie stood and stretched. It had been a slow day, even by Silver Quill standards. Granted, living in a small town in Kansas could do that. There were often slow days. But today seemed especially slow. Her homework, which hadn't even been started when she arrived, was now nearly completed. While the couple meandered to some of the personalized items with first names

1

already on it, she wiped down the counter. Pumpkin and cinnamon permeated the air from the candle warming next to the computer, bringing autumn indoors in a way the drizzle streaking the windows couldn't. She heard the woman sigh, "They never have our little girl's name."

Wanting to help, Allie walked over. "Oh? What's her name?"

"Jessica."

Allie blinked aqua blue eyes and glanced at the rows of jewelry boxes. "I'm pretty sure we've got a Jessica in there. If not, it wouldn't take me long to engrave a blank one for you."

"Oh they have Jessica, but it's not spelled right."

"How should it be spelled?" Allie asked, a bad feeling she wasn't going to like what she heard settling in her stomach. They already had two spellings of Jessica, one with the traditional double 's' and one with a single 's' for more trendy parents.

"G-Y-Z-Y-K-A. Gyzyka."

Reminding herself that it was not her place to correct a proud parent's spelling, Allie tried to unclench her teeth. "Would you like one of these for Gyzyka?"

"How long would it take?" the man asked.

"About fifteen minutes. There's a toy store just down the

2

block. Perhaps while you pick out a nice teddy bear or something, I can get this done for you."

He eyed her suspiciously. "You? Aren't you a little young to be handling this sort of thing?"

Raising an eyebrow, Allie replied, "I happen to be twenty-one. Just because I look young, doesn't mean I am."

The man shuffled his feet uncomfortably and then asked, "And it doesn't cost extra, does it?"

Allie shook her head. "Nope, same price."

"We'll take it," the woman replied eagerly. "Now, can you also do her middle name?"

"Yes. Let me get a piece of paper and you can write her name down for me. That way I'll definitely spell it right." Allie nearly choked on the last word. She grabbed a writing pad and pen for custom orders and handed it to the dark-haired woman. It was soon returned to her and the couple walked toward the door. As soon as they left the shop, Allie allowed the frown tugging at her smile free. She hated creative parents. Did they have any clue how awful it was to be a child with a weird name? She glanced down at the paper. Gyzyka Mairee. "Looks like they took the vowels from one name and tossed them into the other," she muttered. "Poor girl. Maybe someday she'll change it."

Allie sighed as she began working. She knew what it meant to have a weird name. In elementary school when the other children were learning to write their easy, five-letter names, she was desperately trying to write out the twenty-letter monstrosity her mother had cursed her with. Allisatravondarestra Jones. She supposed she should be grateful her mother hadn't inflicted her with a middle name. Lord only knew what the woman would have chosen. As it was, she'd come home in tears and informed everyone she was going to change her name to Allie because it was short and easy to spell.

"Someday you'll appreciate your name," she remembered her mother saying.

"No I won't! Not ever! I hate my name!"

Her father smiled. "When your last name is Jones, you have to do something to stay ahead." When she didn't return his smile, he added, "It's not so bad. No one will think you're a plain, ordinary Jones. You're going to be special."

"I don't want to be special."

Despite her mother and grandmother pleading with her, Allie dropped the last sixteen letters of her name and replaced them with an e. At least, at school she did. Though she was determined to change it legally on her eighteenth birthday, it hadn't happened. Her birthday had fallen on a Sunday that year, so the courthouse was closed. The legal forms she'd printed and filled out had mysteriously gone missing and then her car died, having never had any sort of problem before. Her grandmother had shown up at the corner when she decided to walk the six miles to the courthouse and demanded to have a talk with her. "You can't legally change your name."

"I can so. It is well within my rights. I've checked it out."

"I'm not talking about rights or what you should or shouldn't do. I'm saying you *cannot* change your name. It is impossible."

Allie scoffed. "That's ridiculous, Grandma."

"No, it's true," Grandma insisted. "Your name cannot be changed. The harder you try, the more challenging it will become. Someday you'll understand."

"Look, Grandma, in some places I already have legally changed it. I go by Allie. I sign everything as Allie. I don't even tell anyone my full name, so everyone I know thinks I'm Allie. All that's left is a formality."

"Precisely. I don't care if you wish to have a nickname. Nicknames are good. They will protect you. But you cannot change your name. It is woven into your very being. Trust your old grandmother on this one. Stop trying to formally change your name."

Allie frowned again as the memory faded. Something in how her grandmother had said those words made her pause. She'd returned home and after a few more failed attempts to make things work her way, she quit trying. She only wrote out her full name when required to do so. Most of the time it didn't bother her and she didn't think much of it. As soon as she started a new class, she arrived early and told the professor that she went by Allie. Most would look at the name on their roll sheet and with wide eyes quip, "I can see why." Then she'd watch in delight as they crossed out her name and penciled in 'Allie' next to it.

She heard the shop bell tinkle again and looked at the engraving. It had turned out rather nicely, though she still thought those parents ought to be sent back to kindergarten for a reminder in English phonetics. Carrying the finished jewelry box with her, she walked out with a pasted smile only to see it wasn't the couple she expected. A tall, blond young man was standing near the front desk watching the security cameras."Welcome to Silver Quill Gifts. Can I help you with anything?" Allie asked as she set the box down on the counter and stood next to him.

"Maybe. I'm looking for an Allie Jones."

"Well, you found her. What can I do for you?"

The young man reached around her and wrapped her face with a handkerchief. As she struggled to get away from him, she heard him whisper, "Sleep."

Chapter 2

"What happened to her?"

"Is she going to be okay?"

"Should we call an ambulance? We should. I'm going to call an ambulance."

"No, really, that's not necessary. She'll be fine."

The voices sounded fuzzy around the throbbing in her head. Allie's lashes fluttered and as she came to, a pair of honey-brown eyes looked back at her. She didn't recognize the young man crouched next to her.

"What did I tell you? She'll be fine," he said, turning with a smile to the couple who'd ordered the jewelry box earlier.

"But, what if she hit her head on the floor?" the woman

asked. "I really think she should see a doctor."

Allie couldn't stand people talking about her like she wasn't there. She pushed herself up and snapped, "*She* will take care of *herself* thank you."

"Don't try to get up too fast," the young man said.

She shoved him out of her way and stood, wishing she'd listened as the room swayed precariously. Gripping the counter for support, she tried to remember how she'd ended up on the floor.

"If you're feeling better, would you mind ringing up our order? Then we'll leave so you can rest and take care of the spill on the floor," the woman said.

"Spill?" Allie looked absently at the tile beside her. A small pool of water glistened. Water she knew hadn't been there before. "How did that get there?"

"You must have knocked something over," the young man suggested. "Then you probably slipped on it and knocked yourself out."

"No." Allie shook her head. "No, that guy who came in. He drugged me."

"What guy?"

"Should we call the police? Oh my goodness, you could have been kidnapped!"

"Dear, I'm sure she's fine. Probably just imagined him," the woman's husband said after seeing the young man tap his head. "Miss, the order?"

Allie rang up the jewelry box, her hands numb as goosebumps crawled up her arms. She knew she hadn't imagined anything. Once she was alone, she should call the police. "Have a nice day," she said out of habit.

"You take care of yourself," the woman replied, patting her hand as though she were a sick child. "Don't be afraid to call the doctor."

She smiled. "Thank you, I'm sure I'll be fine."

The couple left and she realized the young man was still standing nearby watching her. "How do you feel?"

"Violated. I didn't imagine anyone. Whoever that guy was, he was here and he drugged me."

"I know."

"What do you mean you know?"

"I know because I came in just as he was preparing to carry you off."

"And you didn't think maybe you should call the police?" Allie snapped.

"They won't find him."

"How do you know?" When he shrugged, she rolled her

eyes. "Well, I'm going to call the police. Somebody needs to do something about that creep."

"Someone has already been dispatched. Trust me, the police won't find anything, so don't bother calling them."

"There's a security camera over there. They'll be able to at least get a look at him and I can give them a statement."

"The footage won't help them."

"Why not?" she demanded, folding her arms over her chest.

He gestured to the computer. "See for yourself."

Allie glared at him, but sat at the computer and pulled up the camera's footage. She watched the couple exit the store and then herself walk into the backroom with the jewelry box. "He should be showing up any minute now." To her astonishment, the blond young man never appeared. Instead, the footage showed her coming out of the backroom and slipping on the floor. She paled. "How is that possible?"

He shook his head. "I'm afraid I don't have time to explain that right now. For the time being, you will be placed in protective care…"

"What?" Allie's voice sounded shrill, even to her. Panic and anger built within her. "What are you talking about? How did he alter the camera? That isn't what happened."

"Allie, I know you're scared."

"I'm not scared, I'm ticked."

He nodded with a shrug. "A reasonable response. Come, I need you to follow me."

"Follow you? In case you weren't aware, I'm at work," Allie retorted with a glare. She didn't know who this guy was, but she wasn't going to follow him anywhere. Not when she was becoming angrier and more confused by the moment. "I can't leave until my shift is over."

"It's over now. I've arranged everything. You don't work here."

Allie slapped him, fear and rage flowing through her. Despite a red mark appearing on his cheek, the young man looked completely unfazed. "Get out and don't come back," she growled. "I've got to figure out what's going on and finish *my* job."

He shrugged, dark hair brushing his shoulders, and sat down.

"Did you hear me?" she asked, desperately trying to keep her voice even. "Get out."

"I can't leave without you. That's *my* job. If you insist on staying here, I can rearrange things, but you're not making things any easier on yourself."

"Just who do you think you are?"

"Dez Polanski, Fairy Guardian," he replied with a slight bow.

Allie blinked. "Fairy guardian?"

"Are you surprised?"

"You're telling me you protect mythical creatures?"

"Just because most people stopped believing in them doesn't mean they no longer exist."

"You're crazy."

Dez shrugged again. She wondered if that was just his normal response to confrontation.

The bell rang and Allie's employer walked in. She was a short, curvy woman with startling blue eyes and black hair. "Allie, just thought I should check in on you. How are things going today?"

"Just fine, Tallia," she replied, deciding not to worry her boss with the disappearing would-be kidnapper. "A couple special ordered one of the jewelry boxes."

"Special order? Didn't we have their name on hand?"

"Not the 'right' spelling."

Tallia chuckled and then saw Dez sitting in the corner. A frown replaced her easy smile. "What are you doing here?" she demanded.

Allie watched in surprise as Dez stood and dusted himself off with a hint of a bow. Tallia had never spoken that way to a customer before. Not even the one who claimed she'd left etching fluid on an item and burned a hole in his car's leather seat.

"She's been found out, Tallia. I have to get her to safety. But she refuses to listen to me."

Tallia turned to Allie. "What actually happened today?"

"It's nothing…"

"Look at the footage tapes."

Allie scowled at Dez while Tallia walked to the computer and pulled up the footage. She paused at Allie's slip and tapped the screen with a silver pencil. The screen blurred for a moment and then the scene replayed as it had actually happened. Allie saw the blond young man enter the shop and then his attempted kidnapping. The footage scrambled as Dez entered the shop with a flare of light. Tallia took a sharp breath. "This is not good."

"Who was he?" Allie asked.

"A hunter." Dez replied.

"A bounty hunter. If he was just a hunter he wouldn't have bothered trying to take her away," Tallia murmured. "Someone must want her for something." She turned to Allie.

"You need to go home. Pack a few things and then go with Dez. He can take you to safety."

"What is going on?"

"How much do you know about your heritage?"

"What?"

Dez paused as though listening to something outside. "Tallia, there's not time. I'll explain as much as I can to her on the way."

She nodded and handed Allie her silver pencil. "Dez will bring this back to me, if I don't see you myself soon, but for now it will protect you."

"A pencil?"

"Hey, it's silver," Tallia retorted with a slight smile. "Go on and be safe."

Chapter 3

Dez led Allie outside. She took a deep breath of the air, musty with the scent of earth and fresh rain. Dez stopped next to a beat-up junker. "Get in," he said, opening the passenger door.

She wrinkled her nose. "I'd rather drive myself."

He glowered at her. "If I'm supposed to keep you safe, you're going to have to trust me."

"Why should I? I don't even know you."

Dez gave his signature shrug. "Tallia trusts me."

Allie couldn't argue him there. Tallia wasn't the type to just trust anyone. Still, this whole situation made her feel edgy. "At least let me drive my own car. You can follow me to the apartment and then I'll go with you in whatever you call that thing."

"It's a car," Dez replied slowly, as though maybe Allie wasn't the brightest bulb.

Not to be outdone, she retorted in the same tone, "It's a rust bucket."

"Hey, this old rust bucket has saved my life a time or two." He patted the top of the car. "She didn't mean it."

Allie rolled her eyes. "Oh yes she did. Is it a deal or isn't it?"

Dez ran a hand through his hair and sighed. "Fine, drive your own car to your apartment. Then you'll have to leave it." He turned away from her, muttering under his breath about stubborn elves as he walked around the car to the driver's side.

Did he seriously just call me an elf? Shaking her head with a frown, she walked to her own car, a beautifully restored '69 Stingray. As a high school freshman, her father had told her he'd match her savings to get any car she wanted after graduation. She'd fallen in love with classic cars watching her parents' favorite movies and decided right away she knew just what she wanted. Dad laughed at first when she revealed her plan saying she'd never be able to save enough. But with a lot of hard work, and a stroke of very good luck, Allie met her goal. She turned the ignition and listened to the engine purr before glancing in her rear view mirror. A smug grin replaced her frown at the look of shock on Dez's face. Revving the engine, she pulled out onto the road and drove to her apartment building.

The drive did little to settle her nerves. Here she was, driving home in the middle of a workday and about to allow a complete stranger to take her no one knew where because her boss agreed that a bounty hunter was after her. It wasn't like she'd ever committed a crime. She certainly wasn't a lost princess or celebrity. She was just an ordinary girl, despite what her father might believe. But the memory of Mr. Creeper whispering, "Sleep," in her ear couldn't be erased. Even thinking about it made cold shivers race down her spine, causing goosebumps to dance up her arms. How had he known her name? And why on earth would he want her?

On arriving at the apartment complex, she checked to see if Dez had arrived. He was stopped at a red light. She pulled out her phone and called the one person who wouldn't call her crazy.

"If you're selling anything, I'm not interested. And no, I won't donate to your phony charities."

"Nice to chat with you too, Grandma," Allie teased.

"Allie, darling, so sorry, dear, but those vultures seem to call every ten minutes."

"Caller ID would mean you wouldn't have to answer them," Allie reminded her for what was probably the millionth time. "Listen, Grandma, is there something I should know about our, um, heritage?"

It was quiet and Allie wondered if the phone had disconnected. Finally her grandmother asked, "What happened?"

"I'm not entirely sure, but this guy claiming to be a fairy guardian or some such thing is making me leave work. Tallia even agreed to it."

Grandma sighed. "I hoped it wouldn't happen this soon. This fairy guardian, what is his name?"

"Dez Polanski, I think. Should I trust him?"

"Only as far as he keeps you safe," Grandma said slowly. "Dez is not a fairy I'm familiar with."

Allie felt herself pale. "You mean, this is real?"

"As real as you and I, darling. I'll meet you at the safe haven. And if you're not there within an hour, I'll call in back-up."

"He says I have to leave my Stingray," Allie said, unable to keep the pout from her voice. She'd worked hard for that car and wasn't about to give it up. Not without a fight.

"I'll have it transported to the haven. For the time being, you would be safer going with Dez as he knows where he's going. Did he give you a staff?"

Allie glanced at the pencil she was given. "Tallia gave me a silver pencil."

"Even better. Be very careful with it and use it only if necessary."

Dez tapped on the driver's window and scowled at her. Allie held up a finger. "Dez is here, I've got to go."

"Be careful, sweetheart. I'll alert your father."

After hearing the phone disconnect, Allie placed it in her pocket. She had hoped so desperately that Grandma would laugh and say it was a marvelous joke. But her grandmother sounded so serious. She got out of her car and frowned at Dez's glare. "What?"

"Just what were you thinking, making a phone call at a time like this?" he demanded.

"It's a free country and my grandmother deserves to know I'm safe. She said you weren't a fairy she knew."

Color rose in his cheeks. "Spoken like an elitist elf." For a tense moment, neither said anything. Allie wasn't sure how to respond and Dez looked like he wanted to challenge her. Well, she wasn't going to jump into an argument without knowing what she was talking about. Finally Dez cleared his throat. "Nice wheels. '71?"

"'69."

Dez nodded appreciatively. "Very nice. By what magic did you come to own a fully restored Stingray?"

Allie ran a hand down the gleaming blue hood. "Hard work and incredible luck."

"Hmph, no one's luck is that good," Dez muttered.

"Mine is," Allie retorted.

He rolled his eyes. "Let's grab your stuff and get you out of here, before your incredibly good luck runs out." Dez gestured for her to lead.

With head high, Allie walked around the building and up the stairs to her apartment. "So, are you going to explain more about what this is all about?" she asked.

"Not out here, I'm not," Dez spat. "You never know who might be listening."

"Sure I do," Allie replied, trying to keep the frustrated edge from her voice. "Mrs. Lampwick down the hall will be eagerly hanging on your every word. Probably hoping to find you and I caught in some delicious scandal to liven her day.

Tora will be at her boyfriend's house and everyone else is working. But I suppose we wouldn't want lonely Mrs. Lampwick to hear all your little secrets, would we?"

Dez frowned. "You don't understand how serious this is."

Allie shrugged as she unlocked her door. "Hard to understand something I've never heard of before." She held the door long enough for Dez to come in before turning to close it, noting that Mrs. Lampwick's window was open and the older woman was sitting right next to it with her knitting. "Have a nice afternoon, Mrs. Lampwick," Allie called. The woman made a show of being startled, but Allie knew better. She'd learned early on that Mrs. Lampwick was a snoop. Harmless, as she never seemed to share her eavesdropping with anyone, but a snoop nonetheless. "And now, Mr. Tall, Dark and Mysterious, would you like to explain to me what's going on?"

Dez watched Allie pull a small bag out of her closet. "What do you know about your family's history?"

"Not much, admittedly," Allie replied, opening the top drawer of the ancient dresser which had come with the apartment. "I guess I've never really thought about it before."

"Your parents didn't tell you anything?"

Allie shook her head, wondering why they hadn't. Surely

they could have told her something. "No. I suppose it must seem strange. We visited Mom's sisters and her parents. Grandma Jones has always lived close by, so I saw her all the time growing up. Grandpa died before I was born. And Dad was an only child, so there were no aunts and uncles on that side to know."

"Wrong. You father has a twin brother."

Looking up from the stack of shirts she was shoving in the bag, Allie gasped. "What?"

"Your father. He has a twin."

"Why would you know that but I don't?" she asked, her eyes narrowing.

Dez shrugged. "I really don't know. I would think your family would have prepared you better for this eventuality. Apparently they didn't."

"So you're telling me I have an evil uncle tracking me down?"

Surprisingly, Dez laughed. "I would never call Lord Drake evil. Pretentious, maybe, but not evil."

"Is there a difference?" Allie zipped up the bag she'd packed. There were enough essentials in there to last a few days. But after that, she was going to need to come back. She wasn't going to live out her life in some crazy-person sanctuary just because this guy claimed she needed protection.

"There's a world of difference between pretentious and evil," Dez replied. "Now, is that going to be enough?"

"I'm not staying wherever we're going permanently," Allie retorted. "I've got a life, classes to attend, a job to do. I don't care what you say or what craziness is going on. You're lucky it happens to be fall break and I won't be missing anything or I wouldn't go with you at all, no matter what Grandma says. I won't live in the shadows."

Dez sighed. "Believe it or not, Allie, that's what we're trying to prevent."

Chapter 4

Allie watched buildings pass by as Dez drove them down the back streets of town. "There's a lot you're going to have to process in the next few minutes, so pay attention," he said, taking her gaze away from what was going on outside her window.

"I'm listening."

Dez glanced at her before returning his focus to the road. "All right. So, first things first, you're an elf and I'm a fairy."

"Right," Allie retorted, sarcasm dripping from her voice. "Tinkerbell could totally be your cousin."

He rolled his eyes. "She's a pixie, and a fictional one at that. Not even remotely close to the same as a fairy. Suspend your disbelief for five minutes and pretend to understand what I'm telling you."

She glared at him, but nodded. Might as well try to figure things out.

"Pixies, fairies, elves, we're all part of the magical world woven into this one. We've been known by many names, but most call us the Fey. Most of us live among humans without them being any the wiser. They might think we're a little odd, or perhaps even otherworldly, but for the most part humans have no idea we're a part of their world."

"You said for the most part. That means some humans do know?"

Dez nodded. "Yes. There are people like your mother who become romantically involved with a member of the Fey, in which case it is our law to reveal our true identity to them. It's only fair for them to know what they're getting into."

Allie frowned. "You make it sound like a bad thing."

He shrugged as he turned out of town and drove onto a small dirt road toward a large forest. "It can be. Most of the Fey are good, but as with any people, some are not. And there are dangers in our world no longer present in the mortal world."

"What like dragons?" she scoffed.

"Among other things."

"Wait, seriously?"

Dez gave her a long look. "I know this is a lot, but every word I'm telling you is true. So, yeah, there are dragons. And unicorns, brownies, mermaids, and other beings you've labeled as mythical."

"This is impossible!" Allie cried, trying to keep her voice even.

"Nothing is impossible. Improbable, maybe. But not impossible. The world isn't always as simple as we'd like to believe," Dez pointed out.

Allie sank lower in her seat, her arms firmly folded across her chest. "Easy for you to say. I bet you've always known about this stuff."

"Not all that hard to believe since both my parents are Fey. I grew up in this world. I can't say why your parents decided not to tell you about it, but they didn't and here we are." He pulled the car into an old garage Allie would have driven past without a second thought. "The rest of the journey will be on foot. Think you can handle that?"

She rolled her eyes. "Just because I've got a nicer car than you doesn't mean I'm incapable of a little hiking. As it happens I enjoy walks through the woods."

"Good," Dez said, "because that's exactly what we're going to be doing." He got out of the car and Allie followed suit.

The garage he'd parked in was near the opening of the forest Allie had always seen on the edge of town, but been warned against ever going in. She wasn't sure what it was about the woods that frightened her parents, and particularly her grandmother, but she hesitated as Dez walked forward unfazed. "Should we be going in there?"

He turned to her with a mocking grin. "I thought you enjoyed walks in the woods."

"My parents have never allowed me to go here," Allie replied, her voice small.

Dez scoffed. "You're telling me that never once in twenty-one years have you decided to sneak a peek inside? You've never crossed into the forest just to see what was so forbidden about it?"

Allie shook her head slowly, a blush rising in her cheeks.

"Are you serious?"

"It was the one rule they made me promise to never break," Allie retorted, feeling a need to defend her obedience.

"They made you promise?" Dez asked, suddenly looking unsure.

She nodded. "I was four I think, maybe five. But I saw the forest when we were driving somewhere and I asked about it. They wouldn't say much, just made me promise to never go there. And I haven't."

Dez growled and ran a hand through his hair. "This complicates things."

"Why?" she asked. "If you really need me to go into the woods, I'll go."

"You can't. Once an elf gives their word, it cannot be broken. You would have to get permission from the person you made the promise to."

Allie stared at him. "It can't be that hard. People break promises all the time."

"Have *you* ever broken a promise?"

She thought for a moment and realized he was right. Any promise she'd ever made had been kept. Even the one to kiss the kicker on her high school's football team if he managed to make a winning score. It hadn't seemed like a big deal at the time because even though he wasn't a particularly gifted football player, he was cute and a good friend of hers. She figured they didn't have anything to lose by it. Add on top of that it had seemed highly unlikely that such a score would be made. Their team rarely won games and the few times they did score a touchdown, the coach usually had them try for a two-point conversion rather than a field-goal. But at the last home game of the season, being tied up with little time left on the clock, the coach sent Patrick in and somehow he'd kicked the football right through the middle. They'd won the game and Allie gave him the promised kiss.

"Which of your parents made you promise not to go into the forest?" Dez asked, scattering Allie's thoughts.

"I honestly don't remember. It's been years ago."

"Think, because I've got to get you to the haven and this is the fastest way," he retorted.

Allie closed her eyes in concentration, a low humming in her ears.

"Hurry, Allie."

"Shush so I can think." She tried to envision the car ride. Mom and Dad sat in the front seat with Dad driving. Grandma was in the seat next to her booster. Echoes of easy laughter and snippets of conversation crossed her memory. She saw the forest looming on the side of the car. It looked warm and inviting, the leaves changing with the colors of fall. She heard her little voice suggest going there for a picnic.

"You must never go into the forest, Allie," Dad's voice said.

"Why?"

"It isn't safe for you. Promise me you'll never go."

"But, Daddy…"

"Promise."

Allie's eyes snapped open. "It was Dad."

"Great, get back in the garage and call him," Dez replied, pushing her towards the dilapidated building. "We're nearly out of time."

Allie would have protested being pushed around, but the humming had been growing louder. The hair on the back of her neck stood on end as chills swept down her spine. She pulled out her cell phone and dialed her father's number.

"Dorian Jones speaking."

"Dad, it's Allie."

"Allie." Worry and relief colored his tone. "Are you okay? Have you made it to the haven?"

"Yes, I'm okay. No, I haven't gotten to the haven yet. I need you to give me permission to go in the forest."

Dorian sighed. "I can't do that, Allie. The forest is ancient and it's dangerous."

"Dez says it's the fastest way to the haven and there is something out here."

"What is it?"

31

"I don't know exactly," Allie cried in frustration. "When were you planning on telling me about all this?"

He sighed again. "I'm sorry, Allie, you must feel terribly confused. I will allow you into the forest, but only if you follow exactly what the guardian tells you to do. Promise?"

"No, I'm not promising you anything," she retorted.

"I see your guardian explained about that. I will not grant permission unless you make this promise."

Allie narrowed her eyes as darkness fell around the garage. "Technically you already did and I'm taking it. Bye, Dad." She hung up and walked out of the garage, Dez grabbing her hand.

"We need to run. Now."

Chapter 5

Dark clouds gathered above them as Allie and Dez sprinted for the forest. "What's going on?"

"Short story, magic is gathering. The sooner we're under cover, the better," Dez replied.

"Is that why my ears are humming?"

"Yes. Stop talking, run faster."

Allie glared at Dez's back as they continued into the forest. The trees grew dense around them, the leaves rattling in the autumn breeze. Dez ducked behind a thick tree trunk, pulling Allie close to him. "What are you doing?" she hissed.

Dez clapped a hand over her mouth. "Shhh. Just trust me," he whispered.

Allie's heart thundered in her ears as the humming grew and faded like a badly tuned radio. A low growl sounded nearby and Dez turned her slowly toward the tree before pulling Allie closer still. Her breath caught as the growling neared. In a voice so faint Allie could barely tell Dez was speaking, he chanted something she couldn't understand. She felt warm, despite the earlier chill. She grabbed the collar of his jacket and buried her face in his chest, as though not being able to see out would prevent anything from seeing her. He smelled of earth and trees, a spicy note tickling her nose. The steady beat of his heart calmed her and she felt herself relax, despite her fear. Somehow she knew, here in Dez's arms, she would be safe. It seemed forever they stood with Allie's back against the rough bark of the tree, though she supposed it was really only a few moments. Dez relaxed his grip on her and pulled back slightly. "I think we're safe now. The Predator has gone."

She shuddered at the name. "I thought whoever was looking for me wanted me alive."

Dez frowned. "Alive, yes. Unharmed, it would appear, is less important to them. Come, we need to reach the safe haven soon." He took another step away from her and held out his hand. "We're not far."

Allie accepted it as she followed him through the trees. She couldn't help notice the warmth and strength of him. A blush stole over her cheeks as she thought of how close they'd been standing together. What a ninny she'd been! Cowering in his shirt like a frightened child while he somehow kept the creature looking for her at bay. *How did he do that?*

"Glimmer magic," he replied.

She stared at him. "Did you just read my mind?"

Dez chuckled. "No, I'm not that powerful. I don't think you realized you spoke aloud. Anyway, glimmer magic can help mask things, or people, you don't want found. It isn't particularly difficult to perform, but I'm glad it was effective this time."

"Why wouldn't it have been?"

He looked at her with a shrug. "Predators are powerful in their own right. Many can see through a glimmer enchantment. We were fortunate this one didn't."

Allie followed in silence, thinking about what he'd said. "Dez, why are you willing to risk so much to protect me? Wouldn't the Predator have harmed you if found?"

Dez remained quiet and for a moment, Allie thought he'd ignored her. "My duty is to the Fey realm. You are a part of it, even if you hadn't known that before."

"There has to be more to it than that."

Something intense which Allie couldn't identify flickered in his eyes, bringing out golden flecks. "Does there have to be?"

She sighed. "I guess not. I just don't understand why you'd risk yourself for a total stranger."

This time he didn't respond at all, just kept leading her through the trees. Darkness hovered over them and the air became chilly. Gnarled branches reached toward the leaden sky above. Dez slowed as they reached an impossibly tall oak tree. Allie had only ever seen trees this wide the one time she and her family visited Redwood National Park. She would never have gotten her arms around the trunk. She wasn't sure even if she and Dez tried together they'd be able to reach around the mighty tree. Dez released her hand and took out a thin stick Allie hadn't noticed him carrying before. He touched a large knot near the base of the tree and whispered to it. The roots began to writhe and lift, creating a doorway into the tree. "Welcome to the Summer Tree. Through here we can reach the haven without detection from unfriendly forces."

"The Summer Tree?" Allie asked, following Dez under the canopy of roots into a tunnel illuminated by glowing lanterns.

"The original name, Seómar, is very old and after years of

mispronunciation became Summer. But the word it comes from means haven."

"Oh." Allie was silent as she walked through the tunnel, awed by a sight which shouldn't have been possible. Fallen branches, stripped of bark and polished to a sheen, shored up the walls of the tunnel. Brass lanterns with aged glass windows hung from the wall on vine motif hangers. "So, you're a fairy."

"Yes."

"Where are your wings?" Allie asked.

Dez laughed. "I'm surprised you're just now asking that. When we spend time with mortals, obviously certain things have to be hidden. Have you seen *The Lord of the Rings* movies?"

She nodded. "Yeah, my mom loves fantasies."

"Makes sense that she fell in love with your father, then. Well, you know how the elves normally appear just like everyone else, just taller and with pointy ears?"

"Yes, but when they're doing something special they have a sort of glow around them, right?" Allie replied.

"It's like that for us. If I'm doing something that requires a great deal of magic, then mortals directly affected would see me as I truly am, wings and all. But for the most part, I'm your average, run-of-the-mill guy. Just much better-looking," he added with a wink.

Allie rolled her eyes. "You wish."

Dez clapped a hand to his heart. "Ouch, Allie. Come along, they'll be waiting for us."

"Wait, they?"

"The Fey Council. Something will have to be decided for your protection and an investigation begun to learn how you were discovered."

Silence fell between them as they left the tunnel and entered a light-filled grove of trees. The autumn leaves glittered as though dipped in gold and copper. Allie looked around herself in wonder. Compared to the darkness of the once forbidden forest, the glade was ethereal. Deer grazed under the branches without taking second notice of Allie and Dez. Birds flit between the branches and sang to each other. "It's so beautiful here."

Dez smiled. "Let's keep going."

Allie followed him deeper into the peaceful forest. Something about what Dez said bothered her. "Don't you think it's strange that anyone would want to discover me?"

He hesitated. "Some are very interested in Fey folk."

"Dez, you know something you're not telling me. Why

would they look for me?"

"That's not something I can answer, Allie," Dez replied. "It's not that I want to keep you in the dark. I'm truly not the right person to explain it to you. However, all your questions will be answered when you speak with the Fey Council. I promise."

"I doubt even they could answer all my questions. Some of them will have to be answered by my parents. They'll both be here, right?"

He nodded. "And your grandmother. I'm sure she will have immediately gone to get your parents after hearing about your, um, adventure."

Allie frowned. She wasn't sure she would call an attempted kidnapping adventurous, but perhaps she wasn't as outgoing as some. The trees thinned and she saw a castle looming before them. "How have I never seen that castle before?"

"You weren't meant to. Mortals can't see it through the enchantments of Summer Wood."

She glanced at him. "You keep saying mortals. Does that mean you and I aren't mortal?"

Dez shrugged. "We are and we aren't. How's that for confusing?"

"I think I've had enough confusing for one day, thank

you," Allie retorted with a scowl. "Just a straight answer."

Laughing, Dez said, "Well, we don't live forever, so in that sense we are mortal. But we have gifts and magic that regular humans don't have, so in that sense we're not mortal. That's as simple as I can make it."

"So, if I'm an elf, does that mean I have a weird glow and pointy ears?"

"Among other things, yes. But most of the time, people would never notice them."

Allie felt self-conscious all of a sudden. "Have you noticed?"

"Fairy gift, I usually see people for what they are. So, yes, I know what you look like in all your elfin glory."

Warmth crept up her neck. "Great. Even I don't know what that looks like."

Dez chuckled as they approached the shimmering castle. "You will soon enough. And you shouldn't worry. You're beautiful."

The warmth spread and Allie was sure her face had grown as pink as her mother's favorite roses. Determined to ignore her companion, she turned her attention to the castle. Built of sparkling stone, it stood grand and majestic in the afternoon light. The wooden doors had a golden hue and were carved with people she had always thought mythical. Before she could look more at the details, the doors swung open.

"Enter, Allisatravondarestra Jones."

Chapter 6

Allie glared at the dainty woman holding the door open. "I go by Allie."

The woman laughed, her blue eyes dancing merrily. "Yes, I'm sure you do. But here, names are special and yours is of the greatest importance to our people."

Allie turned her glare to Dez who refused to meet her eye. "Why is that?"

"Come, Allisatravondarestra, and you shall learn. Dezydery, you are required before the council as well, please join us."

"Dezydery?" Allie asked.

"You aren't the only one who prefers a nickname," he retorted.

"The two of you can discuss the merits of shortening your names later. Right now the queen and council are waiting for you," the woman chided.

Dez bowed and allowed the woman to lead them. He still hadn't looked at Allie. She turned with a huff and followed the silver-haired woman through the entryway. Long halls split from the entrance while spiraling staircases led to upper levels of the castle. Everything shimmered as though infused with a magic of its own. Allie supposed it could very well have been magical, but tried to keep her focus on where she was going. They walked down a long hallway which ended in a pair of ornately carved doors.

Turning her icy blue gaze to Allie, the woman said, "Please wait here while I announce you." She didn't wait for a response, but left Allie and Dez standing outside the doors.

"What's going on, Dez?"

"I can't tell you, Allie, it's not my job."

"So?"

"The Fey Council will see you now," the woman interrupted, appearing at the door. She opened the doors wide before leading Allie and Dez into the room. A semi-circle of throne-like chairs stood before them, each occupied by someone regal. A deeply tanned woman with filmy, golden fairy wings sat in the center of the semi-circle on the grandest throne, wearing a crown of leaves and berries gilt in gold over her raven hair. Allie tried not to stare at the midnight black unicorn laying at the woman's side. As Allie neared, the people sitting dipped their heads toward her.

"Welcome, Allisatravondarestra, future Queen of the Fey," the woman in the center said.

Allie was certain she'd misheard. "I'm sorry, what? I'm no queen. I'm not even a princess!"

Some looked at her with disdain while others appeared amused. The unicorn barely suppressed a chuckle. "Not a princess indeed," he said, his voice warm and rich.

The woman in the center held up her hand. "Despite what you may believe of yourself, Allisatravondarestra, you are indeed a princess. You were born to be the next queen, a large responsibility for one so young. I am Maivelynn, Queen of the Fey."

"Can I be called Allie, please? Allisatravondarestra is just so, it's just," Allie hesitated, trying to think of a way to express her hatred of the name without offending everyone in the room. "It's such a mouthful."

Many giggled, while one member of the council sputtered

in indignation. "See here, one can't simply go around making demands on the council."

"Silence, Lord Drake," Maivelynn said, her voice gentle but firm. "If you desire to be called Allie, we will respect your wish." She smiled, making Allie feel less awkward. "It is quite a mouthful and I know how difficult that can be. The Fey Council bids you welcome and encourages you to ask any questions you may have in a moment. First, Dezydery, do you have a report on today's incident?"

Dez walked forward and bowed low before his queen. "I do, Queen Maivelynn."

As he talked about what happened at the gift shop, Allie turned her attention to the man Queen Maivelynn had called Lord Drake. He stared at her through cold, dark eyes. His blond hair, streaked with silver, was long and straight. Allie could see the pointed tips of his ears. He sneered at her perusal and she turned away. How could he possibly be related to her fun-loving father? She couldn't think of a day when her father hadn't been smiling or laughing, the fine lines around his brown eyes a testimony to a life of joy. Drake appeared to have swallowed a few too many lemons in his lifetime.

Dez was interrupted when the silver-haired woman who'd brought them to the council strode into the room. "My apologies for the interruption, but Dorian and Gemma have arrived and wish to see their daughter."

"Of course, allow them in please," Maivelynn said. "Please continue your report, Dezydery."

Before she could react, Allie found herself enveloped in her mother's arms. "We were so worried about you," Gemma cried.

"Mom, I'm fine," Allie replied. "Where's Grandma?"

"She's waiting in our suite. We'll talk after the council meeting," Dorian replied.

"Yeah, when did you plan on telling me about all this?" Allie demanded, allowing the emotions of the day to seep into her tone. "Like the fact that you have a brother? Or that I'm some kind of fairy princess?"

"Shhh," Dorian said, placing a gentle hand on Allie's shoulder. "We'll discuss everything later. I promise."

Allie's biting retort was prevented by Queen Maivelynn turning her attention to the family. "Now that we have heard what happened, let's discuss the situation we find ourselves with. Allie, it would be very dangerous for you to leave Summer Wood before we discover who or what is behind this attack. I propose you stay here at the castle while Dezydery leads the investigation."

"With all due respect, Your Majesty," Allie said slowly, "I can't do that. I have responsibilities and friends, I can't just disappear."

"You wouldn't just be disappearing, Allie," Maivelynn replied, her voice calm. "We can keep you safer here with many guardians than a single guardian would be able to in your mortal home. The investigation isn't likely to take long. In fact, I would guess you'd be able to return home within a few days. Dezydery is one of our very best guardians and will lead the investigation as swiftly as is possible, I'm sure."

He nodded.

"I still don't understand. How can I be a princess? My parents aren't royalty, I don't think."

Maivelynn smiled. "While that is true, the role of royalty in our world is something very different from the world you are used to. In the mortal sphere, royalty is dependent on lineage and pedigree. Who your parents and grandparents were has a greater impact on your status than who you are. In our world, the past has very little to do with your future. One is either born royal or they're not. Neither of my parents ruled the Fey Realm. Yet here I am, Queen of the Fey. Someday, when the time is right, you will take my place here. In the meantime, you are free to continue your education and personal pursuits as you choose."

"How can you know I'm royal?"

The unicorn next to Maivelynn chuckled. "It is in your very aura, princess. It showed at your birth and manifested itself through your name."

"I thought I just had an overly creative mother," Allie muttered, then blushed as the unicorn laughed again.

"No, I'm afraid your human mother, while creative and magnificent in her own right, could not have come up with that name on her own. Your name is a part of who you are. It is a part of your destiny as our queen." The unicorn turned to Maivelynn. "I would suggest, my queen, that Allie be given the opportunity to retire with her parents for the present. She no doubt has many questions which they alone can answer for her. Perhaps we can reconvene following supper?"

"An excellent suggestion, Lord Nightwind," Maivelynn replied. "You are all dismissed until after the supper hour. Be here at seven, please." Those seated rose and bowed first to Queen Maivelynn before then bowing to Allie. A blush stole over her cheeks. She didn't think she would ever get used to that kind of treatment. Not when she'd believed her whole life that she was just an ordinary girl. She wanted to talk to Dez, find out how much of this he had already known about her, but he was gone. Before she could think too much about where he might have gone, Queen Maivelynn came and embraced her in a hug that smelled of summer sunshine. "I have waited long to see you again, dear princess," she said, her voice low with emotion. "I wish our reunion could have been under more pleasant circumstances, but I am glad you are here in Summer Wood."

Nightwind approached on quiet, silver hooves. "Yes, little one, it is most pleasing to have you back with us."

"I thought unicorns were white," Allie blurted out.

He chuckled. "A few are. We come in many colors and shapes." Maivelynn put a hand on his neck and he nodded. "Until we meet again, Allie." He followed the queen from the room.

Allie turned to her parents. "So, is he like her pet or something?"

"Certainly not a pet," Dorian replied. "Nightwind is Queen Maivelynn's companion and has been for many years."

"Will I have a companion?"

"Perhaps. Time will tell. For now, let's go to our suite. We have much to talk about."

Chapter 7

As Allie followed her parents through the halls of the castle, she took in the sights around her. Marble statues of lovely women, fairies, elves, and mermaids stood in windowed alcoves. "Who are these statues of?" she asked.

"Each statue represents a past Queen of the Fey. Queen Maivelynn's statue is right at the center. We should walk past it soon," Dorian replied. "Ah, here."

Allie stopped in front of a marble statue set within a tall, stone alcove. Carved vines twirled up the walls of the alcove with various flowers. The queen's statue wore a flowing robe, her wings spread wide behind her. Her hair showed a tendency to curl, the berry and leaf crown atop her head.

While it bore a striking resemblance to Maivelynn, Allie felt it missed something vital. "She's not smiling."

Dorian shrugged. "It's rather like old-fashioned photography. A formal photograph would be taken with everyone straight-faced. Same with the statues of our queens."

"But the queen is almost always smiling," Allie pointed out.

Gemma patted Allie's shoulder. "True, but portraits with smiles can be difficult. Especially when your canvas is stone."

Allie frowned at the statue. "She just doesn't look like herself without her smile."

Laughing, Dorian said, "And you know this after only a few moments with her?"

"The statue should have a smile. It's part of who Queen Maivelynn is," Allie insisted.

Dorian led them further down the hall and soon stopped in front of a large oak door. It swung open and Grandma appeared in the doorway. She took a long look at Allie. "I see you survived your ordeal."

"Obviously."

"Don't be sassy," Grandma chided as she ushered them into the room. She motioned to a sitting area with velvet cushioned settees and armchairs. "Tell me everything that happened," she said as everyone took a seat.

Allie shook her head. "No. First, I want to know why this was all hidden from me. Dez told me the Fey laws say you have to tell people when the Fey realm is going to affect them. I'd say becoming queen of a realm I didn't know existed counts as a pretty big effect."

Gemma took a deep breath. "Allie, dear, our reasons were for your best interest."

"I don't see how hiding my future from me was for my best interest."

"Don't you?" Dorian asked, his tone serious. "Allie, imagine if we had told you from childhood that you were destined to be Queen of the Fey. I realize many little girls dream of becoming a fairy princess, but imagine if you grew up knowing you *were* a fairy princess, or rather, elfin princess. Don't you see the damage that could have caused?"

"You would have told all your friends and as a small child, they might have played along with you," Gemma added. "But as you got older, they would have mocked you."

"And living in the mortal world means acting mortal," Grandma said.

"Then why live there? Why not stay here in Summer Wood?"

Dorian hesitated, his gaze flitting to his mother. "Well…"

"We could not stay here," Grandma interrupted. "Many members of the Fey Council were most displeased when your father married a mortal woman."

"Why should it matter?" Allie asked. "Dez said the Fey become romantically involved with humans often."

"Involved with, not married to," Gemma corrected softly. "Often human/Fey relationships are, well, temporary."

Allie blushed. "Oh. But I still don't understand why they should care. I mean, there were other humans who became Queen of the Fey, right? I saw their statues."

"Yes and no, Allie. Elves, fairies, mermaids, they are all fairly obvious to spot when they are visible as they are. Witches, however, look the same as any other mortal woman."

"Witches? Like, warts and broomsticks witches?"

"Allie, please take this seriously." Grandma frowned. "The Fey realm hosts many different peoples and each of them has a place in our world and in the mortal world. The decision for your family to stay in the mortal world for as long as possible was two-fold. One, the council did not approve of the marriage. And before you get snarky about this being the 21st century," she continued as Allie opened her mouth to protest, "members of the Fey Council have their own laws and regulations to abide by. Your father's decision to marry a mortal went against those laws."

Allie turned to her father. "You were on the Fey Council?"

Dorian smiled, though she saw pain in his eyes. "I was once. Now my position has been given to my brother and he seems to be filling it quite well."

"Yeah, about him. Why did none of you ever mention him? And why has he never visited? Surely you've missed him after all this time."

"I haven't," Gemma retorted, the bitterness in her tone catching Allie by surprise.

Dorian took Gemma's hand and smiled at her before turning his attention to Allie. "Drake made it perfectly clear how he felt about my decisions and our family. We felt it best to keep the distance so perhaps he would realize what he was missing out on."

Allie looked at Grandma. "And you felt the same way?"

"Certainly not the same way Drake felt. I have come often to visit him, hoping he would see past old prejudice for the magnificent woman your mother is. But it seems I have been unsuccessful in my efforts."

"Could he have been behind the attack today?" Allie asked

quietly. "I mean, if he really dislikes mortals that much, he must hate the idea of someone half-mortal becoming Queen of the Fey."

"No," Dorian said fervently. "I'm sure he would never stoop so low."

Grandma nodded. "While he is pompous and stuck in the last century, Drake knows his duty. He also knows the reality is very few of us are pure Fey. After all, those midsummer flings often result in spring babes. To get back to our original discussion, though, the second reason for the decision was to allow you a normal childhood. Living in the Fey realm can be wonderful, it's true, but you will have advantages over your peers with your experiences in the mortal realm. It will make you a better ruler when the time comes for you to take your place as Queen."

Allie was quiet for a moment. "I'm still not sure I understand all of this."

"It will take time," Gemma said, patting Allie's hand. "It took me several weeks to wrap my mind around what your father was and how that would affect me and our future together. But one thing I promise you, your father and I will be here with you for as long as you need us."

"Thanks, Mom," Allie replied with a smile. "How long

have you known that I was a princess or whatever?"

Grandma smiled. "Since you were born. The birthmark on your shoulder told us."

Allie's hand reached for the butterfly-shaped mark she had always been asked to keep covered. "So, then Queen Maivelynn has one too?"

"Yes, though I admittedly don't know where hers is," Grandma replied. "When the midwife saw the mark, she immediately called for Queen Maivelynn to come. It was our queen who could see your name."

"So she's to blame for that?" Allie asked.

"I'm afraid, my dear Allie," Dorian said, "as much as you'd like to place blame for your unusual name on someone else, being a destined queen means the name is yours just as surely as Maivelynn's name is hers. And you should know, your name isn't the longest or the most unusual of the Fey Queens."

"You're kidding, right?"

Grandma chuckled. "No, he's quite serious. Look at those statues again sometime. You'll see their names engraved at the bottom. Some have had beautiful, graceful names. Others, well, others have had more interesting names."

Allie considered everything she'd been told. "Is there

anything else I should know about? I mean, am I still going to be able to live in the mortal world and work there?"

"Certainly," Gemma replied. "Tallia has been keeping an eye on you since you started working for her."

"Tallia is a fairy?" Allie guessed.

"A fairy godmother," Dorian corrected. "She was assigned to you early on, but didn't want to be seen overmuch in your life before you came of age. Her reasons are her own, so don't ask me why. The silver pencil she gave you is her wand. I hope you didn't need to use it."

Allie pulled the pencil from her pocket. "No, and I wouldn't have known what to do with it anyway."

"As I told you on the phone, dear," Grandma said, "had you needed it, you would have known how to use it."

A knock at the door interrupted their conversation. Dorian opened the door and Drake swept into the room. "Well, brother, I see you and mother have come back home at last." He tossed a look of disdain at Gemma. "I see you're here too."

"Of course I'm here," Gemma retorted. "Where else would I be?"

"I'm sure I don't know what you humans do with your days," Drake sneered. He turned his attention to Allie. "And you're the little princess."

Allie thought it rich that he was calling her little as she could now see she stood a few inches taller than he did. "That's right, and I don't believe we've been properly introduced."

"Formal introductions between family members?" Drake arched an eyebrow. "Is that really necessary?"

"We all know how you feel about formality," Gemma said icily. "So how about you humor your niece?"

He scowled. "Very well." Drake dipped into a low bow. "Princess Allisatravondarestra, I am Lord Drake, your uncle."

"I go by Allie, Uncle Drake," she replied. "Nice to meet you."

"The pleasure's all mine," he said, sarcasm dripping from his tone. "And now that we've gotten that out of the way, how about we have a little chat?"

Chapter 8

Allie could think of several things she'd rather do than chat with her snobby uncle, but a glance at her grandmother made her realize perhaps they all needed this. "Very well, Uncle Drake. Won't you have a seat?" Now that they were in the same room, Allie could see similarities between her father and Drake. Both were tall and slender, though Drake was shorter than Dorian. They shared deep brown eyes, though Drake's lacked warmth. And though Dorian kept his hair short, it was the same silver and blond mix as his brother. She wondered if it had ever been difficult for her grandmother to tell them apart when they were younger.

"Thank you," he replied. "It's a shame we had to meet

under these circumstances."

"I think that could have been avoided had you come to visit," Allie said, unable to keep the bitter comment to herself. "Weren't you curious?"

"Hardly," Drake retorted, flicking at invisible dust on his sleeve. "I've seen children before."

Allie glared at him, suddenly aware of a tingling spreading through her body. "Yeah? Well I've seen jerks before too, so I guess neither of us missed anything, did we?"

"Allie," Dorian chided, a warning note to his voice, "that is not how we speak to our elders."

The tingling intensified as she said, "It's not how one should speak to a future queen either."

Grandma came between them and set a hand on Allie's shoulder. Soothing warmth flowed through her, taking away the sensation that had been building. "It's not how family should speak to each other," she said firmly. "Drake, if you've come merely to stir malcontent, I suggest you return to your own suite. This day has been hard enough on our Allie without you making things worse. However, if you have something pertinent to discuss you can do so if you choose to be civil." She frowned at him. "I taught you better."

Drake had the grace to look chastised. "My apologies,

Mother."

"I'm not the one you owe an apology to," she replied.

He swallowed hard, his lips puckering as he turned to Allie. "I am sorry, princess. Perhaps I might explain some of my actions."

"That would be nice," Dorian said.

"I would think it would be obvious to you, brother," Drake replied. "Eliciting strong emotion is the easiest way to determine whether someone is truly Fey or not. Your daughter has quite a strong aura."

Allie scowled. "Are you saying you purposely made me angry just to see if I was really what everyone claims I am?"

Drake looked her over. "I don't suppose it needs to be said, but having one Fey parent doesn't necessarily mean the offspring will be Fey as well."

"Of all the pompous, inconsiderate things to say," Dorian snapped. "You've known she was Fey since her birth. So has every other member of the Fey Council. Why did you even bother coming here?"

"As I said, we need to have a chat," Drake said.

"This has been more like a battle than a chat," Gemma scoffed. "If you want to chat, let's chat." She pasted a smile to her face. "It's only been twenty-one years since we last saw you. What have you been up to?"

"The usual. Overseeing the Fey realm, taking part in Council discussions. I suppose you're still doing your art thing, are you Gemma?"

Gemma frowned. "That 'art thing,' as you call it, is my occupation. And yes, I am still painting. I have an online store which does fairly well. Although, I suppose you don't know what an online store means."

"It means it exists only on a computer," Drake sneered. "Just because I choose to live in the Fey realm doesn't mean I have no idea what's going on in the mortal sphere."

"Could have fooled me," Dorian muttered.

Drake glowered at his brother before turning to Allie, "So, what have you been doing with your life?"

"I'm studying to be a veterinarian."

"Animal doctor, interesting choice."

Allie couldn't tell if he meant that in a good way or not. "I like animals," she said with a shrug. "This will allow me to help them."

"Elfin magic will make that pursuit even easier for you," Drake replied, the merest hint of respect entering his voice. "Now that we have all the little pleasantries out of the way, let's talk about what happened today."

"Why do you care?" Allie regretted the question the moment it left her mouth.

Drake frowned as he turned his dark gaze on her. "Despite the tension between us, Allie, I care very much what happens to members of the Fey. Not only is it my duty as part of the Fey Council, but it is also a personal mission to see to it that our people are safe." He looked at his brother. "All of our people. Tell me everything you remember," he said, turning his attention back to her.

Everyone turned to her and Allie felt small and self-conscious. "It's much like Dez said at the meeting. I was working at the gift shop, a strange young man with blond hair came in and asked for me. I told him who I was and he drugged me somehow. The next thing I knew, I was on the floor with Dez hovering over me."

"Lucky he arrived when he did," Gemma murmured.

Drake shook his head. "Nothing lucky about it. Dezydery Polanski has been Allie's personal guardian for quite some time now. Since she started college, I believe. I'm concerned that this young man slipped through the barriers in place. I will have to speak with the fairy."

"It's not his fault," Allie insisted, though she wasn't sure why she was defending Dez. She barely knew him and apparently he'd been keeping secrets from her. "I'm sure he came as quickly as he could."

"Be that as it may," Drake replied, "I will have to speak with him. If one Bounty Hunter made it through, others will likely discover that opening." His expression softened somewhat. "I don't believe Dez had anything to do with what happened. But for your safety and the safety of the realm, we must explore every option. You say you were drugged. How?"

"He put a handkerchief over my mouth and nose. Must have used chloroform or something."

"No, that's not possible. A synthetic poison like that would have no effect on you, other than an allergic reaction. A blessing and curse of being Fey," Drake said with a small smile. "The hunter must have used either magic or a natural poison. Strong enough to knock you out, but not to kill you." He pulled a handkerchief from his pocket. "Wipe your mouth and nose with this. It may be too late, but it's possible there is enough left on your skin for us to determine what exactly was used. Hopefully then we can have somewhere to start."

Allie did as she was told. "After Tallia came to the shop, Dez insisted on bringing me here. We stopped at my apartment long enough for me to pack a bag, which," she added, "I've just remembered is still sitting in Dez's monstrosity of a vehicle."

Drake chuckled. "I see he hasn't gotten rid of the beast yet. Not surprising. Your things will be retrieved, don't worry. He mentioned in his report a Predator following you into the woods. What can you tell me about it?"

An involuntary shudder wracked through her as she remembered the feral growling. "Not much, I'm afraid. I never saw it. But I could hear a humming noise in my ears and everything suddenly became dark around us, and clouds gathered. It was growling and Dez put himself between me and whatever it was and said he worked a glimmer spell to keep it from finding us." She paused and looked at Drake. "He said most Predators aren't fooled by a glimmer spell, why did it work this time?"

Stroking his chin, Drake said, "Very interesting. He's right, of course. Predators will usually see through glimmer enchantments. My best guess, and without having been there it truly is a guess, is that Dez performed the actual spell but you were somehow able to enhance his power. Did you feel anything during that time?"

Allie blushed, her memory instantly turning to the strength and safety she'd felt in Dez's arms. "Other than terrified?"

Drake gave her a knowing look. "Ah, yes, that would be a

feeling. I meant anything powerful. Something that felt different from usual?"

"I can't think of anything. I felt," she paused, looking for words that wouldn't embarrass her or send her father into an overprotective fit, "warm. Safe. Even though I was scared, I didn't feel like I was in immediate danger. I guess I knew Dez could take care of it."

A trace of a smile lifted Drake's lips. "Then I would say you helped him in that without realizing it. Most interesting indeed." He rose suddenly. "Well, I should get back to my suite and prepare for supper. The queen will undoubtedly desire for you to sit with her, but I hope at breakfast the four of you will consider joining me. Since we're being thrown back together, the wisest thing would be to make the most of it. Perhaps many of us have been too stubborn over the last two decades." He inclined his head. "Until then, princess. Dorain, Gemma, Mother."

As suddenly as he'd come, he was out the door. "Did that make sense to any of you?" Allie asked.

"It's a peace offering," Grandma said with a smile. "I realize, it didn't start out that way," she added as Gemma snorted. "But I believe he came if not to make amends, to make an overture of friendship. Now, Allie, tell me more about this fairy guardian who rescued you."

Allie grimaced, knowing there would be no hiding information from her grandmother.

Chapter 9

Allie couldn't remember ever being in a grander place for supper. Even the fancy French restaurant her parents had taken her to for her eighteenth birthday paled in comparison to Queen Maivelynn's dining hall. Large doorways led out into a beautiful courtyard filled with lovely flowers and graceful statues. In the hall itself, sparkling chandeliers sent rainbows dancing on the walls as the candlelight hit tiny crystals. Golden chairs with velvety cushions invited the guests to relax as they waited for the meal to begin. The queen's table was made of a light colored wood with vines carved up the legs and around the edges. Fine china plates and crystal goblets were set at every seat. When the last guest had entered the room, Queen Maivelynn walked in. Everyone rose as she walked with grace to the head table. "Good evening, friends," she said, her voice warm. "In all things, let us be thankful."

She took her seat and everyone else followed suit. Servants brought in trays of food, serving the queen first and then her guests. Fluffy rolls, green salad, and seasoned venison were served in turn, each course more delicious than the one before. Allie sat quietly, observing the room. Her parents spoke softly next to her.

"What do you think of our home?" Queen Maivelynn asked, breaking through Allie's thoughts.

"It's beautiful," she replied. "I've never seen anything like it before."

The queen laughed. "I'm glad. Someday, this will be your home. I understand from your guardian you desire to return to the mortal sphere as soon as this unpleasantness is ended. Is that true?"

Allie wasn't quite sure how to respond. "Well, yes. There are important things for me to do."

"More important than leading your people?" Nightwind asked from his place at Queen Maivelynn's side. While he had no chair, nor a place setting, Allie had seen a golden bowl on the floor with a silvery liquid which he occasionally drank from.

"I don't think it's necessarily more important," Allie began, "but I want to continue my education and be with my friends. And I don't think I'm supposed to be leading anyone just yet."

"That is true," Maivelynn replied, stroking the unicorn's wavy mane. "It may be a wise decision for you to return to your life in the mortal realm. There is much you can do there while preparing for your duties as Queen of the Fey."

"Preparing?"

"You must learn the ways of our kingdom and the laws that govern us. You cannot lead a people you do not understand," Nightwind said.

Gemma smiled ruefully. "If only people in the mortal sphere believed that."

"Ah, yes, the world would be a much more pleasant place if they did," Nightwind agreed. "Here, it is imperative that you know the different peoples you will be ruling as well as the land itself. There is much for you to learn, little one, but I have no doubt you will learn quickly and well."

"Why do you have such faith in me?" Allie asked quietly.

Nightwind looked at her, his blue eyes kind and warm. "Because you are my future queen. I believe in you just as I believe in my queen Maivelynn. There is great potential in you, Allie."

"I have a weird question," Allie said. "When I first arrived, I was told names were important. When I'm queen, will I have to go by my full name again?"

Maivelynn laughed. "Only when you are doing something official. Even I have a nickname, and my name is not so long as yours."

"Really?"

She nodded. "When I'm not doing official business, I go by May. Not very many know my nickname. Only a select few."

Allie blushed as she realized the queen had trusted her with something special. The meal continued with a peaceful quiet. Maivelynn reminded Allie to come to the council room to continue their meeting. "We need to discuss how to proceed from here. Somehow you don't strike me as the type of person who sits quietly while others are doing."

"What makes you say that?" Allie asked.

Maivelynn smiled. "Because you remind me of myself. And if I were in your shoes, I wouldn't want to sit around while other people figured out what was going on." She rose from her seat and nodded to everyone before leaving the dining hall through a door into a large courtyard, Nightwind following behind her.

Allie turned to her grandmother. "Did she just give me permission to not sit idly?"

"That's exactly what she did," Grandma replied. "I would use it to its fullest potential."

"How?"

"Well," Grandma began with a wink, "you could start by assisting your fairy guardian with his investigation. Two heads are better than one, you know."

Allie shook her head. "Grandma, I'm not sure what you read between the lines of our discussion earlier, but there is nothing there. I just barely met him, for crying out loud."

Grandma laughed. "Once is all it takes, Allie. And truly, I think it would be good for you to join him. There is something unusual in how all this happened. I think between the two of you, you could probably figure out what is really happening."

Quiet for only a moment, she eyed her grandmother. When Grandma refused to meet her gaze, Allie said, "You have a theory on what happened, don't you?"

With a sigh, Grandma nodded her head. "I do."

"Are you going to tell me about it?"

"No, love, not unless I feel it absolutely necessary to do

so."

"Why not?"

"Because for your sake, I pray I am wrong."

Chapter 10

Allie walked with her grandmother to the council meeting. Her parents went to their suite and said they would talk with her afterward. Grandma had tried to go with them, but Allie insisted she join her. "You might need to share your theory with the Council. Or at least with Dez. It might give him a starting point."

They entered the council room and Allie noticed extra chairs had been set up. "We thought you might prefer not to stand the whole time," a fairy said as she curtsied.

"Thank you," Allie said. "The chairs will be very appreciated."

Smiling, the fairy curtsied again and left the room.

Allie sat in one of the chairs, surprised by how soft it was despite being made from wood. She ran a hand along the arm of the chair. The smooth birch felt warm under her skin. She turned to Grandma. "How old is this chair? It feels so soft and warm."

Grandma chuckled. "Oh, who knows? I would guess it's older even than I am."

Others entered the room, taking their seats in the semi-circle reserved for the Fey Council. Allie leaned to Grandma. "How can I know what type of person they are?"

"Look closely," Grandma whispered. "Concentrate. Then you will see them as they are, if they have in fact kept their aura hidden. Most Fey do not hide within our own realm, with the slight exception of mermaids out of water, but that is understandable. It is generally only in the mortal world we mask our identities."

Allie saw that Grandma was right. It was easy to identify the fairies by the large, filmy wings sprouting from their backs. The elves were tall, their ears pointed, with an air of magic about them. Two women appeared normal at first glance, but a closer look revealed fish tails. "Mermaids!" Allie gasped.

Grandma hid a smile behind her hand. "Of course. There

are members of every Fey people in the Council. It's the best way to find out what everyone needs."

"I suppose I shouldn't be surprised."

"Hardly. This is all new to you." Grandma paused for a moment as Allie frowned at her. "I know you're still upset with us about that, but we truly thought it would be in your best interest," Grandma said gently.

Allie wasn't sure she was ready to forgive them for the secrets they'd kept. Would it really have been so bad to grow up knowing she would rule a kingdom someday? Most princesses actually knew about their heritage. She could suddenly empathize with Sleeping Beauty when she'd been told, "Oh by the way, you're a princess. Happy birthday!" At least no one had ruined her birthday, yet. There was still time for that as her birthday wasn't all that far off. Her thoughts were interrupted as those already sitting rose to their feet. She scrambled to follow suit as Queen Maivelynn entered with Nightwind. Not far behind them, Dez strode into the room with Tallia.

As everyone else resumed their seats, Tallia enfolded Allie in a tight hug. "Are you all right, my dear?" she asked.

It took a moment for Allie to find her voice. Tallia's looks had changed dramatically from that morning. Her black hair was streaked with blue and silver. Filmy blue wings fluttered behind her. She wore what could only be described as a princess gown of blue and silver taffeta. She looked far more like a princess than Allie did. "Um, yeah, I'm fine."

Tallia smiled. "That's a relief. And you still have my pencil?"

Allie held the silver pencil out to her. "Turned out I didn't need it after all, but thank you for letting me borrow it."

In Tallia's hand the pencil shifted and grew until it became an eighteen inch wand tipped with a sparkling crystal star. "I'm glad you didn't have to use it, Allie. And I'm even more glad that you're safe." Tallia patted her shoulder and then took a seat on one of the extra chairs.

Dez gave her a curious look. "Hanging in there?" he asked. He looked the same as he had in the gift shop when she'd come around. She tried to focus on him, but something about him made it difficult. She still couldn't see what he looked like in his fairy form.

"Well, I've had more surprises than I ever wanted in one day," Allie admitted, "but I'm still here."

He grinned at her, one corner of his mouth quirking higher than the other. "Well, I'm glad you didn't try to run off. It would make my day more difficult, that's for sure."

Allie nodded and sat down as Queen Maivelynn called the room to order.

"We still have much to discuss in regards to what happened to Princess Allie this afternoon," Maivelynn began. "First, Lord Drake, please report on what you learned from Allie and Dezydery."

As her uncle stood, Allie glared at him. Had his overture of supposed peace merely been a ruse so he could gather information? She felt her grandmother's hand on her knee. Glancing over, Allie saw her barely shake her head. She knew Grandma was right. She shouldn't assume the worst of her uncle, especially since she really didn't know him all that well. But it was hard not to feel bitter as Drake skimmed over what they had discussed. "It is my opinion, Your Majesty, based on what has been reported that someone was trying to prevent Allisat-, erm, Allie, from discovering her true identity. Why else would they attempt to kidnap her while she was still unaware of the existence of our world?"

"Wait," one of the mermaids, an athletic-looking woman with deep brown hair, interrupted, "are you saying the princess had no knowledge of the Fey realm before today?"

"My parents raised me in the mortal sphere," Allie replied. An anger and resentment from earlier surfaced as she continued. "This might have been avoided had my father not been removed from the Council simply for falling in love with and marrying my mother."

"Allie, that is not something for you to question," Maivelynn said firmly. "What is past, is past. And there is nothing we can do to change it. Yes, Lady Marissa, it is true that until today Allie did not know the reality of our world. However, I suspect she was given more information about us than perhaps she realized in the forms of stories and legends."

While she wanted to argue, what the queen said was true. Her parents had told her fairy tales from her earliest memory. When most kids were spending their summers lazing around and getting bored, Allie spent her summers delving with her parents into old legends and tales. Every vacation took them somewhere she was encouraged, and indeed expected, to allow her imagination to run wild with thoughts of legendary creatures and mythical beings. She glanced up again when she heard her name. Everyone was staring at her. Heat flooded her face as she said, "I'm sorry, I think I missed the question."

Queen Maivelynn frowned, her tone chiding as she said, "We were proposing an investigation be conducted by Dezydery Polanski. As he is your personal guardian, it is up to you to allow him to temporarily relinquish that duty in preference of discovering who and what is behind today's occurrence."

Allie glanced at her grandmother and then at Dez. She didn't want him far from her. Something told her she would be in greater danger without his presence, even if she had a hundred guardians take his place. "No, I will not allow him to relinquish that duty," she said, trying to keep her voice steady despite her nerves. "However, I would like him to lead the investigation. Two heads are better than one," she added, remembering what her grandmother had said at supper. "With all due respect to the Council, I ask to join him."

Chapter 11

Chaos erupted as Council members argued among themselves and with her.

"You can't possibly be serious."

"What does a princess know of investigations?"

"Out of the question."

"Think of the danger!"

"Do you want the enemy to be successful?"

"Queen Maivelynn, you can't!"

Allie felt the tingling within her grow as the shouting reached a fever pitch. "Enough!" she yelled, rising to her feet. Everyone stared at her and she could feel power surging through her. "While I am asking for permission, understand I will go without it. I am Princess of the Fey," she said, pausing to look each Council member in the eye. "I have responsibilities to my people and to this land. Responsibilities I can't meet if I don't understand what is happening and why after twenty-one years I'm suddenly in danger. Dez has been faithful in his guardianship and I will not have him replaced. However, he is also better qualified than anyone else to lead the investigation which leaves me in quite a predicament." The tingling began to fade and she realized she had probably made some horrible breach in protocol. A hot blush crept up her cheeks. "I apologize, Queen Maivelynn. I believe I spoke out of turn." She sat down and tried her best to be invisible.

"You are forgiven," Maivelynn replied, her tone bemused. "Allie is correct. Two heads are better than one and Dezydery has never failed in keeping the princess safe. However, it is a risk. A risk which may not be worth taking"

To Allie's surprise, Drake stood. "If I may, Queen Maivelynn, based on the reports I received from both parties involved in today's incident, I think Allie's suggestion has merit. A Predator has powerful dark magic. They are not easily fooled, even by the most experienced guardian," he explained. "Somehow Dezydery and Allie were able to combine their powers. I can't explain how as I was not present for the event, but it is the only way a simple glimmer enchantment could have fooled a Predator. Perhaps working together, they will be able to find answers faster than if Dezydery were to go alone. As for Allie's safety, I believe the Council can approve some additional safety measures for her protection. And as Allie pointed out, Dezydery has been a faithful guardian, never allowing her to fall into harm's path until today. With how everything happened, I sense there is something afoot here that will not come to light easily." He looked at Allie and a small smile twitched his lips. "I approve of Princess Allie's proposal and give her my blessing."

An ordinary looking woman on the right side of the circle shook her head. "This is not going to end well," she said. "I understand Allie's concern, I truly do. But to go off with no real understanding of the dangers she is facing is foolhardy at best."

"I don't know that it's fair to say she has no understanding, Lady Hazel," Marissa replied, fingering the shell necklace she wore. "However, I agree that this seems a foolish plan. Wouldn't it be better to keep the princess here where she can be kept safe and start learning about this world she will be leading?"

The debate continued for some time between the council

members and Allie forced herself to remain calm. Maivelynn turned to Dez as the last member gave their opinion. "I find it interesting, Dezydery, that you have made no comment about Allie's proposal. You've never been one to shy away from a debate. What are your feelings on the matter?"

He stood slowly and bowed low before the queen. "I mean no disrespect to any member of the Fey Council, but I feel many here underestimate our princess greatly. Yes, she has much to learn, but she is also tenacious and skilled. I've been observing her for a few years now and feel that her request is not only warranted, but necessary. I would be glad to have her accompany me on the investigation. Many of you would do well to remember that for the most part, we will be traveling in parts of the Fey realm, giving Allie an opportunity to see what she will one day rule. It also gives her an opportunity to observe the people she will have responsibility for without their knowing her full identity. I'm sure, Queen Maivelynn, you would agree that this could provide her with many unexpected benefits." Maivelynn nodded and Dez continued, "I have successfully kept Allie safe from many dangers and Lord Drake has stated how we were able to deceive the Predator sent after her. If it is my queen's will, I will continue my guardianship of Allie while together we investigate the meaning of what has transpired."

Maivelynn gave one of her summery smiles. "Very well. I believe we have discussed the matter to its fullest. It is my desire that Allie and Dezydery indeed work together on this investigation as swiftly as possible. This council will reconvene in three days' time to discuss what, if anything, has been discovered and what we plan to do from there. Go, Allie and Dezydery, with the blessing of the Fey Council. Meeting adjourned."

There was some grumbling as those who had opposed got up to leave. Hazel walked to Allie and Dezydery, twisting a red curl around her finger nervously. "Please come to my chambers before you leave. I know things the Council does not and it would be best that you proceed with that information."

"Why did you not bring it up in the meeting?" Dez asked, his eyes narrowed.

Hazel looked at him. "There are many reasons, the primary being I do not wish to have my people brought under condemnation for something which may or may not be related to one of us."

"You believe a witch could be to blame?"

"I'd truly prefer to discuss this in my chambers where

there are fewer listening ears," Hazel replied, glancing around.

Allie blinked at the lovely woman standing before her. "You're a witch?"

Hazel smiled, her green eyes twinkling. "Of course. You didn't really think witches were just about warts and broomsticks, did you?"

Blushing, Allie asked, "How did you know I said that?"

"Witches have exceptional hearing and I happened to be in the hall walking past your suite when you made your comment," Hazel shrugged. "Don't worry. I am not offended, princess. However, I would request that the two of you join me before breakfast. I will give you what information I have. Hopefully it will be of some help to you." She turned away, her green gown swirling about her as she walked out of the room.

Soon Grandma was at Allie's side again. "Well, dear, you certainly took your royal role seriously this evening."

Allie looked down with a sheepish smile. "I guess I should have kept my temper in check."

"No," Grandma countered, "I think the Fey Council needed to see that. They needed to be reminded that you aren't just some random elf. You are the very future of our world. Come, there is much to do before you leave."

Allie nodded and turned to where Dez had been standing, but didn't see him. "How does he do that?"

"Do what dear?"

"Always disappear before I can talk to him."

Grandma laughed as she led Allie from the room. "My dear, Dez is used to staying in the shadows to keep you safe. While you are now aware of him, for the majority of his career, you haven't been. It's probably somewhat of a habit for him to move out of sight before he's noticed. And it is still his job to protect you. He's probably checking perimeters or whatever it is guardians do."

"I guess," Allie replied. But she couldn't help feeling disappointed. She'd hoped to talk with Dez about their upcoming assignment and find out how she could best help him. Now that she was going to be part of the investigation, she felt a desperate need to prove herself not only to him, but to the Council.

Chapter 12

Allie struggled to fall asleep, despite the splendor of the room she was in. After filling her parents in on the meeting and what was decided, Allie worked with Grandma to sort through her few things to determine what would be most important to take with her. Then everyone had left her on her own so she could rest. Allie snorted. It would have been hard enough to rest just with an attempted kidnapping. Now she'd suddenly found out about a whole other world that one day she was going to be responsible for. A world someone for some unknown reason, didn't want her to know about. The weight of her task weighed on her mind, refusing to allow rest to enter. She walked to the open window and looked out into the inky black sky. Stars sparkled and danced overhead while the moon glowed in a crescent of silver. Night blooms filled the air with their perfume, putting Allie in mind of summer more than fall. Somewhere an owl hooted and the faint sound of singing played in her ears. Movement nearby caught her attention and Allie strained to see what it was in the darkness. A figure lurked near the trees and Allie's heart began racing. What if it was another bounty hunter? She shrank away from the window, trying to decide what she should do. Grabbing the brass lantern by her bed, Allie pushed it out the window to illuminate the yard. "Who's out there?" she called.

"Just what do you think you're doing?" a voice hissed.

"Dez?"

"Who else would it be?" he asked, coming closer to the open window. The lantern light gave a golden glow to his face, highlighting the bronze streaks in his dark hair.

Allie put the lantern down on a nearby table. "How should I know? I thought maybe you were a bounty hunter or something."

Dez snorted. "And if I had been were you planning on throwing your lantern at me? Wouldn't have done you much good."

She scowled at him. "I don't know, but what were you

doing skulking in the shadows?"

"First of all, I don't skulk, and second, I was doing my job."

"Skulking in the shadows?" Allie retorted.

"Keeping you safe," Dez replied.

Allie was quiet for a moment. "Isn't that what you do during the day?"

Dez shrugged.

"Don't you ever sleep?" she asked, her tone softening. "Surely even fairy guardians get tired." The fear of being kidnapped past, Allie looked at Dez. His earthy brown clothes were perfect for keeping hidden and brought out the brown hues in his eyes. He looked enchanting under the starry sky, the glow of moonlight highlighting his features. The moonlit scene from Romeo and Juliet came to mind and Allie quickly pushed the thought away. The last thing she needed was to be distracted by romantic thoughts.

"My first duty is your safety. Sleep is overrated," he said.

Allie shook her head with a laugh. "You're not going to be much help tomorrow if you don't get plenty of rest. You said yourself I would be safe in Summer Wood. Go get some sleep. We'll both be better off if you do."

"Would you believe me if I said I tried and couldn't?" Dez

asked.

Knowing she was only awake because sleep eluded her, Allie nodded. "Yes, I'm having the same problem."

Dez looked at her for a moment. "Can I join you?"

"Sure, though I'm not sure how I'd get you in here."

"Now you're underestimating me," Dez said with a teasing grin. He climbed up onto the windowsill and sat on it. Silence fell between them as they looked over the garden. "It's a lot to process for you, isn't it?" he asked, turning to her.

"Yes, but it's not just that," she admitted, taking a seat next to him on the windowsill. "I feel like my whole world has been pulled out from under me. Everything I thought I knew doesn't seem to add up with what my reality is. I know my parents thought they were doing what was best for me by hiding all of this, but I can't help thinking they made a terrible mistake."

"Maybe they did," Dez said candidly. "But they were doing it out of love. It may be hard to see now, but perhaps there will be good to come from not knowing ahead of time."

"I guess," Allie replied. "So, you've always lived in the Fey realm, always known about it. What can you tell me?"

He chuckled. "I could tell you stories to make your worst nightmares seem tame." She stared at him in shock and he grinned. "I could also tell you stories to make your wildest dreams seem possible. The Fey realm is magical and that has both good and bad qualities. I suppose it's not unlike the mortal world. There seems to be a mix of good and bad there too."

"That's for sure," she agreed. "I guess there isn't a magical place where everything is always wonderful, is there?"

"Just Summer Wood," Dez said, looking around the peaceful garden. "Here things always seem to turn out right."

Allie thought about what he'd said. "Dez, do you think that might be part of why whoever was behind today wanted me kidnapped before I found this place?"

He thought quietly. "It could be. But why? What do they gain?"

"You said the Fey realm can make your worst nightmares seem tame. If someone wanted me to fear my role as future Queen of the Fey, and they kidnapped me to someplace dark and terrifying..." Allie's voice trailed off as the implication of what she'd said hit her. "Why would I ever be willing to take my place here?"

Dez ran a hand through his hair. "A good point. If you were terrified of what you thought was the Fey realm, you might be willing to take steps to ensure you never have to accept your role. That's a very interesting thought. It could mean there is someone who wants to usurp your authority."

"But why wait so long? I mean, I'm not the queen now. And Queen Maivelynn appears to be in excellent health, so I can't imagine I'll be taking that role any time soon. In some way wouldn't it make more sense to go after her and then just let me be. After all, I didn't know about any of this until today. If they removed the queen, they could simply take her place and I would never be the wiser."

Shaking his head, Dez said, "No, that wouldn't work. For one thing, the Summer Wood is too heavily guarded. A direct attack on the queen would take more power than any one Fey has. For another, if something happened to Queen Maivelynn you would be summoned immediately. Whether you'd known about us or not, you would have found out. But, if they had captured you and you relinquished your claim to the throne, that would throw off the balance of the Realm. Being Queen of the Fey is something you are born to do. If you were so badly traumatized that you gave that up, it could have a butterfly effect of sorts which might put the queen in danger, allowing for an easier overthrow."

Allie shivered. "That's just scary."

"It is scary," Dez admitted. "But, there's nothing to say

your theory is correct. We will have to consider it as a possibility though."

"That's not very comforting."

Dez put his arm around her shoulders. "That's why I'm here. To keep you safe and let you know you won't have to face any danger alone."

She gazed up at him and smiled. "Thanks, Dez. That makes me feel much better, truly."

He took her hand and kissed it. "Well, princess, it's time you got some sleep. Don't fear for tomorrow." Without warning, he disappeared into the darkened garden.

A glow of contentment settled over her as Allie slipped down from the windowsill and walked to her bed. With Dez's promise in her heart, Allie soon fell asleep.

Chapter 13

Allie jolted awake in a cold sweat. Her heart raced as she tried to settle her breathing. The fleeting images of her nightmare disappeared, leaving her disoriented and confused. Golden rays of sunshine poured through the open window, chasing away the darkness her dreams had brought in. Songbirds twittered in the trees and the heady fragrance of flowers filled the room. Allie took a deep breath and closed her eyes. "It was just a dream," she murmured. "Just a dream." She got out of bed and shivered slightly as a cool autumn breeze played with the gauzy curtains of her room. An old-fashioned basin with water and a washcloth sat waiting on the dresser. Allie splashed water on her face, banishing the last remnants of her fears, before changing into fresh clothes for the day. Someone knocked on her door. "Come in."

Grandma appeared with Dez at her side. "Good morning, Allie dear. I hope you slept well."

"Well enough," Allie hedged, unwilling to talk about the nightmares which had plagued her, in part because she couldn't remember enough to talk about them anyway. She looked at Dez who looked perfectly rested. "You look like you slept well."

"I always sleep well in the Summer Wood," he replied. "I just came to see if you were ready to meet with Lady Hazel. She asked for us to be there before breakfast."

Allie grimaced. "I'd forgotten. But yes, I'm ready." She followed Dez out of her family's suite, noting with some amusement the way her father glowered at Dez.

Once they were out of earshot, he asked, "Did you sleep at all last night? You look exhausted."

Glaring at him, she said, "I was hoping it wasn't that obvious."

"'Fraid so, Allie. Are you okay?"

She sighed. "I had a nightmare last night. And before you ask me about it, I don't remember much of anything. I just remember being terrified of something, I don't really know.

It's probably just stress from everything going on, right?"

Dez shrugged. "Sure." He turned left down a hallway and knocked on the last door.

Hazel opened the door. "Good morning, Princess Allie, Dezydery. Please come in." She stepped aside so they could walk in. Allie noted strings of drying herbs tied in the windowsill of the room while a fluffy white dog trotted over to greet them. "That's Mystic. She's quite friendly."

"A dog? I've always thought witches had cats."

"Usually black ones right?" Hazel winked as Allie stammered. "I'm allergic to cats, so I needed a familiar who wouldn't aggravate my allergies."

"Familiar?" Allie asked.

"Sometimes called a spirit guide," Hazel said. "To be brief, a familiar helps me in my magic and generally keeps me company. Mystic is the perfect companion. She's sweet and loyal and more helpful than some might realize. Anyway, I'm afraid most of what I have to tell you isn't going to be pleasant," she said, waving at a few chairs which instantly arranged themselves around a small table where a pot of tea and four teacups waited. Hazel poured tea for each of her guests before pouring some into a cup and setting it on the floor for Mystic to lap at. She then poured a cup for herself, took a sip, and continued, "I have observed recently in the Hollow that there seems to be quite a bit of discontent."

"Do you know what it stems from?" Dez asked.

"Yes and no," Hazel replied slowly. "I know some is due to the dispositions of those complaining. There are always those who will see the negative before the positive. But I've noticed many people speaking of," she dropped her voice to nearly a whisper, "her."

Allie blinked. "I'm sorry, who?"

Hazel looked at her and sighed. "I should have remembered you wouldn't know. Nyx," she whispered.

Dez sucked in a breath. "You're certain?"

"Positive," Hazel said. "I think most of them are just latching onto the most recent gossip without thought of the potential consequences. However, I believe there might be some who are truly upset by how her reign, erm, ended."

"Can you explain a bit for me please?" Allie asked, trying to be more gracious than she felt. She was tired of not understanding what was going on.

Hazel sipped her tea and said, "It's been many, many years, princess. I'm sure there are many parts of the Fey realm that do not remember Nyx's rule over us. But, I will explain as best I can. As you know by now, being Queen of the Fey is something you are born to do regardless of who or what your parents are."

"And there have been many different types of queen," Allie remembered.

"Yes. Nyx was the first witch to be queen. However, you won't see her statue in the hall. She was a cruel woman and caused untold problems for the Fey realm."

Dez leaned over to Allie. "The biggest and most well-known being the Salem Witch Trials."

"I always thought that was just people being panicky and superstitious."

Shaking her head, Hazel said, "Oh no, it was not nearly so simple as that. See, Nyx didn't only create problems for our world. She used her incredible power of influence to create problems in the mortal sphere. Most who opposed her found themselves accused of witchcraft by the mortals."

"So, those people really were witches?"

"Some," Hazel replied. "There were also fairies and elves, and a mermaid if I remember correctly. Unfortunately, many were just mortals who refused to accept the demands she was placing. The Fey Council was nearly powerless to stop her."

Allie frowned. "Why? I mean, there would be more of them than her."

"Yes, but she was very gifted with persuasion charms. It was difficult to get enough Fey Council members to oppose her before she had them silenced. It wasn't until they learned she was trying to find a spell for immortality that they united against her. But by then her power had grown so immense, it wasn't certain the Fey Council could defeat her. It was actually a mortal woman working with a fairy which finally brought about Nyx's demise. I won't go into the unpleasant details, but once she was gone, her influence died as well. The Fey Council determined that all memory of Nyx, other than that which must be kept to prevent repeating the same mistakes, be erased. Her statue was destroyed and the next queen was given stricter charge concerning the Fey realm. Unfortunately, since then witches have been looked upon with distrust, despite the next witch queen being a kind and benevolent woman."

"That's not fair," Allie cried.

Hazel eyed her for a moment. "What is fair? Fair is something you should expect from sporting events, not life. And there are many among my people who would agree with you. That is why I wanted to warn you of what I've heard. There have been whispers of someone trying to find Nyx's spell book. If they found that, they might be able to find her notes on immortality."

"But true immortality is impossible," Dez said. "Isn't it?"

"Who am I to know?" Hazel asked. "It is a forbidden subject of study and so I have never looked into it. However, I can see the appeal; especially to someone who thought that would bring them the respect they feel was lost after Nyx."

"That was hundreds of years ago," Allie said slowly. "Why would it matter now?"

Hazel took a deep breath. "It was rumored that Nyx had a child. There is no confirmation, of course, but the rumor still exists. This would not be the first time revenge was extracted long after the initial offense was committed. And it would not be the first time the descendants of a past queen would feel entitled to the role."

"Thank you for the information, Lady Hazel," Dez said, rising from his seat. "This will certainly give us something to consider as we begin our investigation."

"One last thing," Hazel added as they walked to the door. "There is someone you should speak to as soon as possible. She lives in the mortal world, but might have more access to gossip than I do. My position on the Council means few are willing to speak to me directly about what is being said. However, I always find the best information when I speak to her. I would suggest you meet with her to find out what other rumors might be circulating."

"Who is she?" Dez asked.

"Cynthia Lampwick."

Chapter 14

It was mid-morning before Dez and Allie were able to begin their journey. Queen Maivelynn had requested a private meeting with them to discuss her concerns and to give last-minute counsel before they started. Allie's parents wanted to say their goodbyes before heading back home. Several members of the Fey Council also had bits of advice they wanted to share. When Dez led Allie out of the castle she asked, "So, what's our first stop?"

"Well, first we'll go to one of my contacts and see if she can help us find out what you were poisoned with. Then we'll go speak to Cynthia."

"Do you think Cynthia is my nosy neighbor?"

Dez grinned, "Are you sure you want to call someone you know can turn you into a toad 'nosy?'"

Allie gaped at him. "She wouldn't do that, would she?"

He gave his characteristic shrug. "You never know." They soon walked to a stone archway which led to a dark tunnel. Dez turned to her and said, his tone serious, "Where we're going, you need to stay close to me. Not all Fey are good and this is a less-than-savory part of the realm."

"Then why are we going there?" Allie asked.

"Because we need information and this will be the best place to get it. Just stay close and keep your head down."

Allie nodded and followed close behind him as they entered the tunnel. Every so often, a lamp shone dimly in the darkness. The walls glistened with drops of water while dirt and grime filled in crevices between the stones. "Is it meant to be forbidding?" she asked, her voice echoing around her.

"Only to those who wouldn't want to be caught in the dark," Dez replied. "Some people like scary tunnels."

"People like you?" she retorted.

"Nope. I'll be glad when we're on the other side," he said honestly. "We're getting closer."

Allie could see sunlight marking the end of the tunnel. She and Dez moved more quickly as they neared its warmth.

When her eyes adjusted to the brightness, Allie gasped. "Are we still in the Fey realm?"

Dez chuckled. "Yes, but like I said, this a less-than-savory part. Stay close."

Allie didn't need told twice. The trees here grew together in gnarled clumps, what few leaves they had were withered and dry. Mist curled around the trunks and her feet. She recognized a few plants growing nearby and moved closer to Dez to avoid them. The last thing she needed was a case of poison ivy while she was trying to help Dez with the investigation. She looked around at the buildings. Most were built of dark brick or stone, ivy climbing up the sides. They passed various shops until Dez stopped in front of a tall stone building with large windows. She read the sign above the door. "The Green Villain?"

"Saving the planet so you can rule it," Dez finished with a grin. "Yeah, some villains are really into being eco-friendly."

"Seriously?"

He shrugged as he opened the door, a bell chiming above him. "What's the point of taking over the world if it's in such a mess you can't enjoy it?"

"That's our philosophy," a blonde young woman wearing shell bracelets and a sea-blue dress said as she stepped forward with a smile. When she saw Dez, she pounced on him with a fierce hug. "Dezy, darling! Oh, I haven't seen you in ages. Keeping yourself in plenty of trouble, I hope."

Allie's jaw clenched so tightly she worried she might crack a tooth. Who did that girl think she was to throw herself on Dez that way? It didn't help that Dez didn't seem to mind. Was this his girlfriend? She supposed she really didn't know that much about Dez, but the thought of him being with someone like the giggling girl before her soured her mood.

"Who's your sidekick?" the girl asked, catching Allie's attention.

She started to answer, but Dez said, "Oh, she's not a sidekick, Twyla. Just a very good friend." He gave Allie a dazzling smile that melted her insides. But along with it was an unspoken warning. He didn't want her saying who she was. Didn't bother her any. It was probably better people not know who she was.

Twyla glanced at Allie and her violet eyes flashed. She turned back to Dez with a full-lipped pout. "Moving on already, Dezy? Shame." With a dramatic sigh, she asked, "What can I do for you today?"

Dez handed her a handkerchief. "I need to know what is on this."

"Dust?" Twyla replied with a sweet smile.

"Not likely," he retorted.

"Impatient today, aren't we? Have somewhere better to be?" Twyla gave them an interested glance and Allie sensed it was more than just interest in her companion. "Let me take it back for some tests. It may take a while. Feel free to look around. Maybe you'll find something to keep you here for a little longer." She sauntered out of the room with another simpering smile at Dez.

"What was that all about?" Allie demanded in a strained whisper.

"I'm sorry, but if we have any hope of finding out what was used by that bounty hunter, Twyla is our best source of information," Dez replied.

"She certainly seems to know you well," she added, annoyed by the irritation in her tone.

He laughed. "I come here often when on assignment. Good source of gossip. Pretend to be interested in the wares. If we don't at least look at something, Twyla will get suspicious. But don't touch anything. They cater to villains, remember?"

Allie nodded and began wandering the aisles, staying within sight of Dez. A sign boasting organic herbs, essential oils, and poisons hung over a line of shelves. Hemlock, nightshade, eye of newt, mistletoe, and other dangerous plants were arranged neatly in jars and baskets. She walked past ground-collected gemstones, mermaid-safe puffer fish and lionfish, but paused at one sign. "Ethically collected dragon scales?" she asked.

Dez moved to her side and looked at the basket of multi-colored scales. "Yeah, that means some poor fool went into a dragon cave and collected scales from the floor that had already fallen off. Dangerous work. Dragons are rather partial to their scales and don't part with them willingly."

"Even the ones they've shed?"

"Especially those ones. They know their scales have magic properties and dragons don't like to share anything. Somewhere around here there are ethically collected unicorn horns too."

Allie gasped. "How can you ethically collect a unicorn horn?"

He shrugged. "Find a unicorn that has already died, I guess. It's a tricky business, and I wouldn't be all that sure that anything in here is as ethical as it might claim."

"Villains?" Allie guessed.

"Something like that," Dez replied with a lopsided grin. "Oh, here are their wands and staffs. Sustainably sourced, hmm. I wonder just how many fallen logs there are for them to collect from." He glanced at her. "I'm sure you see things like that in the mortal world too."

She rolled her eyes. "Going green is all the rage."

He looked at her curiously. "Not necessarily a bad thing."

"Not when it's done properly, I suppose," Allie admitted. "It just gets irritating after a while. One can only do so much, right? And we can't do all that much about the generations before us."

Dez nodded. "Yeah, even the Fey leave a mark on the world. I suppose the best we can do is hope our mark leaves things better rather than worse."

"I wish more people said it that way. It wouldn't come off so grating or self-righteous."

He chuckled. "Maybe I should be their spokesman."

Allie giggled, imagining Dez on a "Save the Earth" type commercial. "I think you better stick with what you're doing. You're good at it."

Twyla appeared, her make-up obviously touched up. "Good news and bad news. The bad news is your sample was absolutely awful and I had a rough time finding anything on it."

"So what's the good news?" Dez asked her.

She flashed a brilliant smile at him and flipped a blonde curl over her shoulder. "Just that I'm amazing and I was able to trace the ingredients. Someone concocted a rather powerful sleeping charm. Whoever was hit with this is probably still dreaming of their Prince Charming coming to their rescue. You haven't been getting into too much trouble, have you Dezy?"

Allie glanced at Dez, her heart racing. What did that mean?

"Interesting," Dez said slowly. "What are the ingredients?"

Twyla handed him a slip of paper. "It's all written down there. We do sell that particular potion, but no one has bought any in months. I would guess this was homemade."

"You don't suppose you could share the name of your last customer with me, could you?"

She wagged a finger at him. "That'll cost you extra, darling."

Dez pressed a handful of coins into Twyla's hand and kissed her cheek. "For old times' sake?"

Twyla sighed. "Well, if that's the best I can do. I did happen to glance at the books and the last person to purchase it was," she paused with a wicked grin, "Lady Hazel Lornpielo."

Chapter 15

If Dez was surprised, he didn't show it. Allie tried to keep her face unreadable as Dez said, "Thanks for the information, Twyla."

"Anything else I can get for you today?" she asked.

"I don't think so. Trying to keep a budget, you know," Dez replied with a wink. "We'll see you around."

Twyla waved them from the shop. "Ta-ta!"

Allie waited until they were back to the tunnel before saying, "Are all mermaids that flirtatious?"

"Twyla's not a mermaid," Dez replied. "She's a siren. All of the water Fey tend toward being flirty, but sirens are particularly notorious. Of course, they're also more dangerous than mermaids."

"How can you tell the difference?" she asked. "Twyla seemed very similar to Lady Marissa, at least from what I could see."

He shrugged as they walked. "It takes time and practice. Some of it is the very fact that Twyla lives in a darker part of the Fey realm. Mermaids don't like darkness. They prefer sunny beaches and warmth."

They walked in silence for a moment before Allie asked the question burning in her mind. "What did you think of Twyla's revelation?"

"Which one? That you should still be waiting for Prince Charming?"

Allie sighed. "I guess that one too. Just how potent was the poison she told you about?"

"Hard to know," Dez admitted. "If it was indeed homemade, there is a distinct possibility the ingredients weren't quite mixed properly. There's also the fact that I arrived when I did. While the potion immediately knocked you out, the hunter wasn't holding it to you long enough for you to go into a deep sleep. And, of course, you are Princess of the Fey which gives you a certain amount of power, even if you aren't totally aware of it. But without an exact breakdown of the formula, I just can't know for sure."

"Isn't that what Twyla gave you?"

"No," he replied with a scowl. "She gave me an ingredient list. It's obvious she was trying to hide something about it from me. Unfortunately, there won't be a good way to find out what exactly she's hiding."

Dez's statement reminded Allie of their conversation with Twyla about the last customer. "Why do you think Lady Hazel bought the potion?"

"She didn't. It was a lie."

Allie gaped at him. "How do you know?"

"Twyla's eyes flashed," he replied. "It's a tell-tale sign that a siren is lying. Or unhappy." Dez looked at her for a moment. "Thinking of which, she didn't seem thrilled to meet you."

Not about to admit the feeling was mutual, Allie said, "Yeah, I guess she thought I was encroaching on her territory."

Dez chuckled. "Probably."

"So then, you two are an item?" she asked, hoping she sounded casual.

"If by item you mean we're somehow involved with one another, only in Twyla's dreams," Dez retorted. "Courting any Fey on the darker end of things would be detrimental to my career. Courting a siren would be a death sentence."

"You mean you'd lose your job?"

He shrugged. "Among other things."

Allie stared. "Are you saying she would actually kill you?"

"You've read Greek mythology, Allie. I think we both know what sirens are like. Eventually, Twyla would tire of me and that would be the end of it. Oh she might keep me around for a while, but it wouldn't last."

She shuddered. "That's awful!"

Dez shrugged again. "That's reality in our world. Honestly, most sirens prefer casual flirting to anything more serious and lasting anyway. Anyway, to get back to Lady Hazel, I don't think she's responsible for what happened. But someone wants us to think she is. The real question here is, why?"

"I don't know."

"I don't either. That's why we're going to go pay your neighbor a visit," Dez replied. "If Lady Hazel is right about her wealth of knowledge and gossip, we might be able to figure out why someone would attempt to frame her for your attempted kidnapping."

~*~

Allie could hardly believe how ordinary her apartment complex looked after spending a day in the Fey realm. The faded red brick showed age and wear, but no magic like the polished marble of the palace. She walked the familiar steps to the building, As usual, Mrs. Lampwick had her window open and was sitting near it. A black cat sat on the sill, twitching its tail. Its pale green eyes focused on Allie and the cat mewed as Dez and Allie approached Mrs. Lampwick's door. "Come in, my dears," she said before they could knock, not bothering to look out her window. "I've been expecting you."

Dez opened the door and held it for Allie, tipping his head in a slight bow. She frowned at him. She didn't want him treating her like a princess. If she were honest, she would admit she wasn't sure how she wanted anyone to treat her. But a pampered princess was not who she was and she knew that wasn't how she wanted to be perceived. Dez bowed to their hostess. "Good morning, Mrs. Lampwick. I assume you are Cynthia?"

"You assume correctly," she replied with a wrinkled smile. "However, I wouldn't make a habit of assuming anything. We all know what happens to those who assume."

Allie couldn't help a giggle. Her father had told her that more times than she cared to remember when she was young. She took a few moments to observe the woman before her. Cynthia looked every bit the loving grandmother with her powdery blue hair twisted in a loose bun at her neck and plump figure. Her hazel eyes were sharp and attentive. Allie was certain nothing got past Mrs. Lampwick.

"You're here to talk about the rumors in the Haven, is that correct?" Cynthia asked, breaking through Allie's thoughts.

"Yes, we are."

Cynthia rocked back in her chair and the cat hopped down from the windowsill and into her lap. She stroked its inky fur and said, "Yes, the rumors are flying rather thick and furious. Happens at times amongst our kind. We like to gossip," she confided with a wink. "Hazel asked me to fill you in on what I know. Few of my acquaintances realize how close she and I are."

"How close are you?" Allie asked.

Beaming, Cynthia replied, "Why, Hazel is my cousin, twice removed. We are also very close friends. But when she was called to represent us on the Council, she and I thought it best to minimize our contact in the Fey realm so people would still be confident gossiping with me. Not all gossip is true, of course, but if one listens closely one can learn a great deal from it."

Dez nodded. "And what have you learned recently?"

"Ah, are you sure you and Miss Allie wish to find out?"

Cynthia asked, sitting forward as the gold flecks in her eyes seemed to glow.

"We need to find out what's going on, Mrs. Lampwick," Allie said. "Please tell us what you know."

"Cynthia to you, my princess. No need to be formal with me," she replied with a kind smile. "Very well. I shall tell you what I've heard and what I've guessed. I'm afraid though, my dears, it's not going to be pleasant."

Chapter 16

Cynthia sat back in her chair, the rockers creaking with age. Her cat dozed as her hands ran across its fur. "I suppose the reality is there have always been rumors about Nyx and what she caused among our people. She had the potential to be a great queen, to lead the Fey into a more prosperous time. You see, what many forget is that those times weren't just dark for mortals. They were dark for us too. Disease, dangers, and of course mortal superstitions, made life difficult for the Fey. Many among our own saw Nyx becoming queen as a way for those troubles to be put behind us. For a while, that seemed to be her goal. She worked tirelessly to set up an agreement with the great dragons, she set trade agreements with the merfolk and sirens, why she even set up the path for them to be able to join us on land in our councils. She wasn't all bad, though unfortunately that is all that is remembered. Yes, Nyx had great potential." Cynthia shook her head with a sigh. "But she got greedy. The power went to her head and instead of continuing a peaceful reign, she brought more evil upon us."

"What does that have to do with what is happening now?" Dez asked.

"Patience, young man, and let an old woman tell her story," Cynthia chided. "Here," she rose and went into the kitchen, coming back with a glass cookie jar filled to the brim with a variety of sweets. "Help yourself." She snapped her fingers and a pitcher of milk and three glasses appeared on the table.

"Mrow," the cat complained.

"Oh, I'm sorry, Percy." Cynthia snapped her fingers again and a saucer of milk appeared on the floor.

Satisfied, the cat leapt from his seat and began lapping the cool milk.

Allie bit into a spicy molasses cookie as Cynthia continued her history of Nyx's reign. "I'm sorry she met the end she did," she finished. "It is a terrible thing for a Fey to be erased from memory. And she is not the first, nor I fear will she be the last. However, what she did was beyond repair. I stand behind what the Council of her day chose. Now, to bring this about to today's problems, I'm sure Hazel told you there are rumors that Nyx had a child?"

"Yes, we'd heard that," Dez replied.

"What would you say if I told you this was not just rumor, but fact?"

Dez frowned while Allie sat forward. "How do you know?" she asked.

"Lineage is often a difficult thing to trace among the Fey. It doesn't concern us as often as it does our mortal counterparts. A pity," Cynthia mused. "We can learn a lot from our predecessors. However, I have been doing some research of my own and I am absolutely certain. Nyx had a child, two actually. She had twin girls. Their names were Prudence and Patience."

"Odd names for a Fey," Dez said slowly. "Most don't use virtue names, even then when it was so vital to hide their identity."

"Indeed," Cynthia agreed. "It is my belief Nyx realized her children might be targeted by both mortal and Fey, but especially the latter. She had a plan for their safekeeping, though. Patience and Prudence were placed in a home with a woman Nyx trusted. One who did not know who or what she was. Whether this was because the woman was out so far away from the rest of society or because Nyx cleared her memory is unknown and frankly unimportant. The important thing, is Nyx covered her tracks well enough that it hasn't been until now that this connection has become clear."

"Have you told anyone about this?" Allie asked.

Cynthia shook her head. "No, I haven't. However, I imagine it didn't take long for the mortal woman who raised the girls to realize there was something different about them. It's hard to say much more about them, as there wasn't a lot written and what little I've found has been very vague. That said, I'm certain of two things: Nyx left her daughters something by which they could learn their heritage and at least one of the girls must have had a family."

"So Nyx has descendants in our time," Dez replied.

"Yes. I haven't been able to trace who they are. The rumors in the Haven, while interesting, do not provide a lot to go on. All I know for certain is there is a descendant of Nyx searching for the spellbooks. These would give him or her incredible power and perhaps her notes on immortality. Just because Nyx was unsuccessful, doesn't mean someone else will be. What frightened the Fey most about her research is she got close. Far too close for comfort. I also know there is someone looking to take over the rule of Summer Wood and all the Fey lands from Queen Maivelynn."

Allie gasped. "But why?"

"Not everyone is happy, my dear," Cynthia said simply. "There are some who are very angry, in fact. Much of the damage done by Nyx has had greater effect on the witches of the Fey than on any other group. And the good she brought to the world has been all but forgotten. There have always been those to complain about these seeming injustices, but now there are some taking action."

"What kind of action?" Dez asked, his tone suspicious.

Cynthia sat quietly for a moment. Then she stood and closed the window to her apartment and drew the curtains shut. She sighed and stood there for a long while before turning to them again. Allie felt she'd watched the tender-hearted woman age before her eyes. Her shoulders drooped and her eyes lost their sparkle. She sat gingerly in the rocking chair and Percy hopped back into her lap, purring softly as though to comfort his mistress.

"You must tell them," he said at length when Cynthia remained quiet.

Allie squealed. "Your cat is talking!"

Percy chuckled. "But of course. I normally keep that to myself, especially since we are in the mortal sphere so often. Most humans don't know what to do with a talking animal. Oh if they knew the stories their pets tell." He laughed again before turning his pale gaze to Cynthia. "But you must tell them what you know. It will only continue to hurt you if you don't."

Dez stood and knelt at Cynthia's feet, placing a gentle hand on her arm. "Cynthia, has someone or something threatened you?"

She shook her head. "No, my dear, not me."

"Your cousin," Dez said.

Tears dripped from her hazel eyes. "It is well-known how loyal Hazel is to Queen Maivelynn. My own loyalty is also known, but I'm not a threat to their plans. I'm a rather ordinary Fey living out my life in the mortal sphere. Hazel is not so fortunate. She is close to the queen, both in relationship and in proximity. This botched kidnapping which brought you to a knowledge of who you are," Cynthia said, turning to Allie, "was no accident."

Allie gasped. "You mean, the young man was meant to fail?"

"That is my belief. Though, of course, I could be wrong. But that would explain how Dez was able to prevent you from being taken in the first place and why the Predator couldn't find you. Hazel filled me in on all the details she learned at the meeting," Cynthia added when Dez and Allie looked confused. "Those responsible have set a plan in motion to discredit Hazel. Then any information she would have gained from me or from her own research would have been called into question. Who's going to believe a woman who attempted to kidnap the Princess of the Fey?"

"Cynthia, do you know who is behind this? Even just one name?" Dez asked.

Shaking her head, Cynthia replied sadly, "I've never heard any names mentioned. Those who speak of this plan do so in times of utmost secret. How they haven't noticed a great, bumbling woman like myself walking about is beyond me. But no names have ever been mentioned, other than those they feel are a threat." She pressed a piece of paper into Dez's hand. "These are others who are under threat of whoever is behind this. Take it as soon as possible to the queen so that she can set protections about them. They will start with Hazel and Xylia, as they are the two witches on the Fey Council."

"Thank you, Cynthia," Dez said.

"Yes, thank you for talking to us. I know it must have been difficult," Allie added.

"Don't thank me yet," Cynthia said ruefully. "The hardest part of this journey is upon you. Mark my words, if another attempt is made to take Allie, it will not fail as the first did. You are both in grave danger."

Chapter 17

As they walked down the street to the beat-up car, Allie noticed Dez frowning. Before they'd left, Cynthia handed them a brown paper bag filled with cookies and gave Allie a small, round stone. "Keep this with you and don't let anyone take it from you. This will offer you some protection, should you need it. You'll know how to use it when the time comes."

"You're thinking," Allie said as Dez still had not said anything after starting the car.

"That obvious, huh?" he teased.

"Well, you're either thinking or my mother was right in telling me my face could freeze if I pouted too long."

Dez sputtered, "I am not pouting, thank you very much."

Allie giggled. "Didn't think you were." She became serious when Dez's chuckle was short-lived. "Fill me in. What's going on in that head of yours?"

He sighed. "It doesn't make sense."

"Do you think Cynthia might be lying to us?" Allie asked.

Dez shook his head, "No, she was honest with us. I could tell by her tone and actions. Had she been lying, we probably would never have left her apartment. What I don't understand is why anyone would want to hurt Queen Maivelynn. She's been a fair and just queen, giving extra opportunities to anyone who feels slighted to overcome the shadows of their past. And because everyone knows how the rule of the Fey Realm works, it doesn't make sense to attempt an overthrow. The people behind it wouldn't stay in power anyway."

"Unless I relinquished the throne."

He nodded. "I suppose that's true. So why make a bungled attempt at a kidnapping on purpose? I still don't understand what they've gained by this. That's what I'm trying to wrap my head around. It makes more sense to me that they were earnestly trying to kidnap you and I was faster than they thought."

"What about the Predator?" Allie asked. "Cynthia seems to think that could have been purposely weakened as well."

Dez shrugged, his dark hair brushing his shoulders. "I just don't know. It's possible, but it would be very difficult. And while this has been a shock to you, I don't think that alone would be enough for you to walk away from your people, would it?"

Allie was quiet as she considered. Would she walk away if given the chance? "No," she said at length, "that alone wouldn't be enough to scare me off. In a weird, inexplicable way who I am, what I am, makes sense. It's still a surprise, and I'm not all that certain how I feel about it, but there are so many things which now make sense to me that I can accept it."

"So then why a fake kidnapping?" Dez asked. "What's the purpose? It would take more than circumstantial evidence to convince the queen that Lady Hazel, or any Council member for that matter, was disloyal to her. And it wouldn't take long for an investigation to prove their innocence."

Thinking for a moment, she said, "What if I'm not the actual target? The person behind this is obviously a Fey and would understand how things work in the Realm, as you've pointed out. I know you're assigned to me, but there are other guardians you work with, correct?"

"Of course. There are many of us. Each Council member

has at least one guardian and the queen has four, the most notable being Lord Nightwind," he replied. "While I work mostly independent of the others, there have been times I've been called to assist in other matters. The guardians are responsible for the safety of the entire Fey Realm and all of the people within. We take care of the same kind of things mortal police officers do."

"Like investigations?" Allie prompted.

Dez's honey-colored eyes widened as he looked at her. "Someone wanted to set up a distraction."

Allie's heart fell to her shoes as she nodded. "And they succeeded."

~*~

A sense of urgency pushed her forward as Allie followed Dez through the darkening forest to the Summer Tree. They stopped occasionally as Dez listened to sounds in the forest Allie couldn't identify. She trusted him to keep her safe, but wanted to get to the palace as quickly as possible. Queen Maivelynn could be in immediate danger and there was little Allie could do to stop it unless she reached her before the others did. They had almost reached their destination when Dez paused and pushed Allie against a tree, putting a hand over her mouth to muffle her protest. When she nodded to show she would stay quiet, he moved his hand and put his arms around her in a sheltering stance. He jerked his head toward the Summer Tree, only a few yards away from them. Allie followed the motion and saw a hooded figure standing near the tree. Focusing in like her grandmother had taught her, Allie could see the man was in fact an elf, though there was a darkness about him she hadn't seen around the others she'd met. He turned about as though to ensure he wasn't being watched and Allie sucked in a breath when she saw his face. The young man who had drugged her at the gift shop was standing in front of the tree. She looked at Dez and he nodded silently, confirming that he'd recognized the individual as well. They watched as he entered the hidden tunnel to the Summer Wood.

"We're going to have to go another way," Dez whispered, releasing his hold on Allie.

The breath she'd been holding released and a feeling of disappointment settled over her as Dez moved away from her. "Where should we go?"

"There's another path into the Summer Wood, but it could be dangerous," he admitted. "I'm fairly sure he didn't see us, but that doesn't mean we should count on that."

Allie sensed the inner battle Dez was facing. He was

expected to keep her safe and taking her through the forest wasn't the best option. She placed a hand on his arm. "I trust you, Dez. Wherever you say we need to go, I'll go."

A faint smile quirked his lips. "Well then, princess, let's be off." He took her hand and kissed it. "Stay close."

That was something she could easily agree to. Allie followed Dez, comforted by the warmth of his hand in hers. He paused more frequently, sometimes changing their course and other times ducking behind the trees to wait for an unseen threat to pass. True to her word, Allie followed his lead without complaint. She missed being able to talk to him, but recognized the need for silence as they worked their way through the undergrowth. After walking for what must have been an hour, Dez pointed out a nearby stream. "The mermaid entrance is there," he said, his voice quiet. "Do you swim?"

Allie nodded. Her parents had insisted she begin learning as a toddler.

"Good. We'll use that entrance," he replied, looking back at the stream. "I'm sorry your clothes will get wet, but you have others at the palace you can change into."

She nodded again. "What do I need to do?"

"When we go to the stream, there's a flat stone on the bottom with a mermaid carved on it. Touch that stone and the passage will open for you. Just swim until you reach the end of the tunnel. It's not too horribly long, but you'll want to swim quickly."

Allie took a deep breath. "I'm ready."

Dez hugged her tight for a moment. "Okay, let's…" A sound behind them grew and his eyes widened. "Run, Allie."

"What?"

"Run!" he shouted, pushing away from her. Suddenly Dez morphed before her eyes into a tall fairy with mossy green wings and a long sword in his hand. "Run, Allie, get to the passage!" he called as he ran to the threat facing them.

For a moment, Allie was frozen in place. A dark red dragon was flying straight toward Dez. Her voice barely a squeak, she asked, "Dez?"

"Go!" he bellowed.

Tripping over her feet as flames engulfed the forest, Allie fumbled her way to the stream hoping beyond hope that Dez would be all right.

Chapter 18

The icy water of the stream bit her legs and arms as Allie tried to find the mermaid rock Dez had described to her. She could hear the dragon roaring behind her, but tried to ignore it. Her hand found a smooth river rock with lines carved into it. Looking closer, she saw the carved mermaid. Allie pressed it and was surprised when the river rocks in front of her shifted and lowered as an underwater tunnel appeared. She took a deep breath and threw herself under the water, soon coming up sputtering at the cold. Bracing herself for the water's chill, she glanced where Dez battled the dragon. "Please come back," she whispered, then took a deep breath and forced herself under the water. Eerie blue lights lit the tunnel and

Allie followed them, the strange sounds of being underwater filling her ears. She could hear whispered notes of a song. The words were strange to her, but brought no comfort. Instead they filled her heart with dread. Trying to focus on going forward, Allie kicked past plants that seemed to wrap about her legs and ankles. Her lungs burned with the need for fresh air. She could see the tunnel widening and knew she was close to the end. Kicking harder, Allie swallowed a scream when something grabbed her ankle.

"Going somewhere, little princess?" a voice sneered.

Allie turned to see a dark-haired siren pulling her back. The siren's blue eyes flashed angrily as Allie kicked her hard in the face. Pulling away from the angry siren's grip, Allie put all her strength into moving forward. She reached the end of the tunnel and broke the surface, allowing much needed oxygen to fill her lungs. But she was soon pulled back under. No matter how she fought, the siren was stronger. The siren's claw-like nails ripped at her clothes and scratched her skin as Allie tried to wrench away from her. As she struggled, the siren taunted her.

"You won't survive for long, princess. Just give in. There is nothing for you above the water. Everything you want is here."

Unsure how much longer she could hold her breath, or resist the cold water's sapping of her strength, Allie wished desperately for Dez to appear. She knew he'd be able to help her.

"Your friend can't save you. Not from all of us," the siren jeered. "Give in to the cold. Accept the water."

Allie squirmed and wriggled out of the siren's grasp, ignoring the stinging words she spoke, and fought her way to the surface of the water. She coughed as the air filled her lungs. She moved as quickly as she could to the shore of the stream, now hidden in a large cave. The siren followed close behind her. The tingling sensation she'd felt in her suite when Drake had goaded her and at the Council meeting when she'd claimed her birthright as princess filled her once again. "Leave me!" Allie shouted.

To her surprise, the siren was pushed backwards as though Allie's words had power. She hissed and disappeared under the water.

The tingling warmth she'd felt disappeared and Allie gulped in the air, shivering violently as her wet clothes clung to her chilled body. She knew she needed to get into the palace and get warm, but she didn't know how to get there. Without Dez to guide her, the Fey Realm was as foreign to her as New York City and twice as frightening. "I need you, Dez," she whimpered, curling around herself in a vain attempt to get warm.

A jacket was tossed over her. "Well, wait no longer. The calvary has arrived."

She looked up, her teeth chattering. "Dez?"

He smiled. "In the flesh. At least, I hope so." After helping her to her feet, Dez wrapped the jacket tightly about her and held her close to him. "We need to get you warmed up."

"What about you?" Allie asked.

"I'm about as warm as I want to get," Dez admitted.

She took a closer look and noticed his hair was singed and his clothes bore scorch marks. "The dragon?"

"He won't be bothering us again," he replied. Stepping back from her, he asked, "Do you think you'll be able to make it upstairs to the palace?"

Though she was still chilled through, she nodded. "I'm not staying in here any longer than I have to."

"Did you get through the passage all right?" Dez asked, wrapping his arm around her shoulders as they walked up a wide, stone staircase Allie hadn't noticed when she first entered the cave.

She told him about the siren. Suddenly realizing Dez was

dry, she asked, "Wait a minute, why aren't you dripping wet like I am?"

He shrugged. "I've had my clothing enchanted to stay dry."

"That doesn't explain your hair."

"Part of being a fairy is being somewhat water-proof. After all, my wings wouldn't work as well soaked through. Most of the time when I'm trying to look mortal, I allow myself at become wet. But I figured today the blessings of being a fairy would serve me well. And it's a good thing too, otherwise I wouldn't be able to let you borrow my jacket."

Allie was quiet for a while before voicing the concern on her mind. "I think the dragon was just there as a distraction to make me as vulnerable as possible."

"It's possible, or someone thought one hazard wasn't dangerous enough for you." He gave her one of his heart-melting smiles. "You're stronger than they thought you were, Allie. That's good."

"Or it's going to make them try harder."

Dez squeezed her shoulders before opening the door they'd come to. "Either way, I'm here for you. No matter what they toss at us." His words warmed her heart, though her teeth continued to knock against each other. He led her into the palace and through various halls to the suite she'd stayed in the night before.

Grandma opened the door just before Dez reached to knock on it. "Dear heavens, child! What on earth happened to you?"

"We'll explain later. First, she needs to get changed out of her wet clothes," Dez replied.

Ushering them into the room, Grandma pushed Dez toward a chair before taking Allie into her room. "Strip," she ordered as soon as the door was closed behind her.

Too tired and cold to argue, Allie peeled off her wet clothes. She heard Grandma muttering words over a set of clothing. When the clothes were handed to her, she started dressing, the cloth warm against her skin. "How did you do that?"

"Simple warming spell," Grandma replied. "I'll teach it to you soon. Here." She handed Allie a warm blanket. "Let's go out and sit with Dez. Then the two of you can fill me in on what you've learned so far. It must be important for you to have come home early. We didn't expect you for a couple more days."

Memory of the young man from the gift shop pushed through Allie's muddled thoughts. "The elf from the shop! I almost forgot, we have to warn Queen Maivelynn!"

Grandma pushed her back as she tried to rush past. "Hold

on, you need to sit and rest. If you go rushing out right now, you're going to just get worse rather than better. Queen Maivelynn is well-protected. Right now, you need to focus on you."

Allie tried to argue, but Grandma shushed her and she sighed, "This is important, Grandma."

"So is your health," Grandma insisted. "Come on, Allie. Come sit in front of the fireplace and warm up. You and Dez can fill me in on what you've learned and then together we can determine what the best course of action."

Allie sighed again. "All right, fine."

Chapter 19

Only once Allie was comfortably situated in front of the fire, with a steaming mug of hot chocolate in her hand, would Grandma allow either of them to start talking about what had happened. Allie couldn't understand how she stayed so calm. She and Dez had just discovered a plot to overthrow Queen Maivelynn, been chased by a dragon, and then Allie nearly got drowned by a siren, and Grandma acted as though they were merely discussing the weather. She hardly reacted to any of the news they shared with her and didn't even blink when they mentioned the young man from the gift shop. "Are you even listening, Grandma?" Allie cried in exasperation when Dez finished reciting what he knew.

"Of course I am, child," she replied. "I suppose I could put on a dramatic show for you, clutch my heart and that sort of thing. But what does that really accomplish? The information you have discovered is grave indeed and the presence of a dark elf in Summer Wood is disturbing. However, if we are to be successful over those who would bring harm to the Fey Realm, we need to keep our heads about us. Now, Cynthia gave you quite a treasure trove of information."

"I'm concerned for her," Dez admitted. "She's heard a lot of things she was likely not meant to hear. I would feel better if she came to Summer Wood where we could keep an eye on her."

Grandma snorted, "Good luck with that. Cynthia doesn't come to Summer Wood often. In fact she rarely goes to the Hollow. She's much happier in her little apartment with that cat of hers listening in on human gossip to bother much with the Fey Realm anymore. I feel certain she only comes when she needs to go shopping for things you cannot find in a regular supermarket."

"If she's there so rarely, how would she have learned so much?" Allie asked.

At this, Grandma leaned closer. "Cynthia has friends who visit her. I'm sure she heard most of the really interesting tidbits when those speaking were unaware of her presence. However, I'm just as certain there are some who visit her and keep her up-to-date on the latest gossip, both good and bad. Cynthia has always known how to persuade people to confide in her."

Dez frowned. "Would she have any reason to go along with a rebellion?"

"Good heavens, no," Grandma replied. "She's as loyal and true as they come. Cynthia would never do anything purposely to harm the queen or any Fey. She is a kind soul, as I'm sure you saw when you visited her."

Allie thought of the large bag of cookies and the stone resting in her pocket. It had dropped to the floor while she was changing and she'd instinctively picked it up. "I have a question. I realize there are good and bad people in the world in general, but it seems that in the Fey Realm, we would have been able to move past this dark and light stuff. Why do we have dark Fey?"

"One might hope such a time may come, and yet the world must always be in balance," Grandma explained. "Just as we cannot appreciate the day without the night, we cannot appreciate the good without the bad. There will always be those who choose to live in shadow rather than embracing the sunshine. And so it is that there remain light Fey and dark Fey. Each of us must make our choices in life. In reality, most of the dark Fey are that way by choice, not by birth. We've all made mistakes, all made poor decisions. Some of which come to the detriment of ourselves and others. We've also made good decisions which have benefited those around us. I believe it is through our choices we can determine how much sunshine penetrates our souls. "

"I suppose that's true," Allie conceded. "Are there any of the dark Fey who participate on the Council?"

Dez shook his head. "No, that has never been allowed. Each of the dark Fey have a light counterpart."

"Like sirens to mermaids," Allie said.

"Exactly," he replied. "They take their concerns to the light Fey in their area and then they in turn bring that information to the Council. We try to make sure we balance the needs of all the Fey people, but it can be difficult. Obviously, there have to be laws in place to prevent harming humans and other Fey, which can be counterproductive to the natural instincts of some of the dark Fey."

Allie considered what he'd said about Twyla. "So, when we were talking earlier about your contact..."

He shrugged. "She's a siren. Despite laws and anything

else, some will still choose to act on their worst impulses. That's why there's a villain shop in existence to begin with. If there were no villains among the Fey, there would be no market for the items Twyla sells." Silence fell over them and Dez pushed at a log in the fireplace with the poker. The flames danced and sparks sizzled at the motion. "I suppose now we have to decide what to do from here."

"That is exactly what we need to do," Grandma said. "Queen Maivelynn does not expect a report from you for another two days. However, I don't believe the information you have should wait that long. Perhaps, at dinner tonight, you could request an audience with Her Majesty. That would let her know you wish to meet with her in private, as well as giving you both some time to rest. An investigation which was supposed to happen over three days has erupted in one. Supper will begin in about an hour. In that time, you should refresh yourselves, rest, and for heaven's sake, child, take care of that burn!"

Allie raised an eyebrow at her grandmother wondering what imaginary burn she'd seen, when she realized Grandma wasn't looking at her. Her eyes were fixed on Dez. Allie followed her gaze and noticed for the first time that Dez's arm had angry red blisters marching over the exposed skin where the shirt sleeve had burned away. "Why didn't you tell me you were hurt?" Allie demanded.

Dez scowled at her. "My job is your safety. Getting you someplace warm was far more important to me than having a Healer poke and prod me."

"Like it or not that's what's going to happen," Allie said, jumping up from her seat. "You're going to get that looked at right now."

"Allie, I can go myself," he argued.

She glared at him. "I'm taking you. Just tell me which direction to go."

He scoffed, "Oh, really? How would you even know I was sending you the right way?"

"Because you would never lie to me," Allie retorted. "Now, the Healer. Where would we find him?"

"*She* is already here," Grandma replied firmly, forcing Allie to return to her seat. She took Dez's arm gently in her hand. "Really, you two, when you aren't behaving like overexcited children you're quarreling like malcontent lovers."

Embarrassment sent flames of pink up Allie's neck and face at the description. "We are *not* lovers, Grandma."

"No, and you're not children either, so both of you calm

down. Wrap back up in that blanket," Grandma insisted, never taking her eyes from Dez's arm. She clicked her tongue. "Didn't have your shield with you?"

"Forgot to get it up," Dez admitted.

"Oh?"

He looked away from Grandma, his face reddening, as she continued to look over his arm. "I was distracted."

A smile flickered across her face and she glanced at Allie. "I see. Well, the good news is I should be able to get this cooled down for you and then wrapped."

"The bad news?" Dez asked.

She sighed, "You're going to have some scarring. If you had shown this to me before we started our little discussion, I might have been able to prevent that too."

"They wouldn't be my first scars," he said.

Grandma chuckled, "No, and I doubt they'll be your last." She spoke soft words and Allie watched as her grandmother changed. Her ears showed their pointy tips and there was an ethereal, golden glow about her as she ran her hand just over Dez's arm. Though she was certain she'd never heard the language before, Allie understood the words her grandmother used. "There now, not quite good as new, but certainly better. Am I right?"

"It does feel much better, thank you," Dez said.

Grandma didn't respond, but rather walked to a nearby table and pulled out a drawer with clean white linens. She wrapped Dez's arm gently. "Keep it clean, young man. You don't want to risk an infection. We're going to need you."

Chapter 20

Allie felt anxious as they went to supper that evening. Dez caught her eye and gave her a guarded smile. *He's right, of course*, she thought as she sat down with her grandmother at the Queen's table. *I need to appear calm.*

"I'm a little surprised to see you tonight, Allie," Maivelynn said after taking her seat. "I thought you and Dez would still be out investigating."

Trying to pick the proper words to form her request, Allie replied, "I'm sure we will be out again soon, however we have learned a few things today which would be best shared immediately."

Maivelynn frowned. "Oh?"

"With all due respect, Your Majesty, this is not the place for such a discussion," Allie said. "Might I beg an audience with you later this evening?"

With a smile, Maivelynn agreed. "No begging required, dear Allie. Come to my chambers this evening after supper. Shall we say eight o'clock? And please bring Dezydery with you. I am most interested in what you have to report."

The decadent meal served to them sated Allie's hunger, but did little to calm her nerves. She found herself scanning the room, looking for the elf she'd seen at the Summer Tree. He didn't appear, but somehow Allie knew he wasn't far away. What had brought him here? She wished she could ask Dez about it, but he wasn't sitting with her. He sat at a table farther away with a group of people Allie hadn't been introduced to. As she focused her sight on them, she saw several were fairies, but there were also a few elves and a couple mermen sitting together. Once again, her focus on Dez did not reveal the earth-toned fairy she knew him to be. She frowned. Why couldn't she see him as he was? She watched a while longer. The group of Fey talked amongst themselves and from the looks on their faces, their conversation wasn't pleasant. She wondered if Dez was filling them in on the investigation, and if so, why?

"He is speaking with the other guardians," Grandma said gently, pulling Allie out of her thoughts. As Allie turned to look at her grandmother, she realized Maivelynn had left the table. "While he will not share all the details with them here, he is giving them enough information for them to be extra cautious."

"That makes sense, I guess," Allie replied.

Grandma studied her for a moment, a smile on her face. "You care very much for Dez, don't you?"

Allie glared at her as telltale color crept up her neck. "What makes you think that?"

Laughing, Grandma said, "You can't hide it from me, Allie. He's been a very good guardian for you. He's kept you safe for us."

"It's not like I ever went that far away," Allie pointed out. "I was still in the same town."

"Yes, but not in the same house. Not even the same neighborhood."

"Everyone grows up eventually."

Grandma smiled. "Yes, I suppose that's true. And we're proud of you, Allie, and all you've accomplished."

Allie returned her grandmother's smile. "Thanks."

"So, just how much do you care for Dez?"

"Ugh, Grandma!" Allie groaned. "Can't I just be friends with a guy without the third degree?"

"Not in this family," Grandma chuckled. "Remember when you were 'just friends' with Cooper Hunt?"

How could she not? No one in the family would let her forget the two years of psuedo-dating with the acne-scarred swimmer. "I will repeat what I know I've already told you. Dez and I just met. We haven't had time to develop anything other than friendship. I don't believe in love at first sight."

Frowning, Grandma said, "You should. That's what brought your parents together."

"Grandma, love takes time. It doesn't happen in an instant. Surely even in the Fey Realm they know that."

"True love takes time, my dear," Grandma admitted. "Real, lasting love takes a lifetime. But you should not completely dismiss the idea of love at first sight. It is in those instant moments of attraction the seeds of true love can be planted."

"I don't think Dez and I are in love," Allie said. "We're friends, almost coworkers at the moment. I don't think there's anything there for you to speculate about." She pushed aside memories of Dez holding her close to shield her from danger and the moonlit kiss to her forehead the night before. She was absolutely not going to share those things with her Grandmother. Those were her memories.

Grandma smiled again, a knowing twinkle in her gray eyes. "I see. Ah well, I suppose there's plenty of time for you to find someone I can speculate about."

Allie laughed, "You're terrible, Grandma."

"Why, yes, yes I am." Grandma winked and then said, "I believe I'll turn in for the night. If there's anything important discussed during your audience, fill me in tomorrow morning. Unless of course Queen Maivelynn sends you and Dez back out immediately, in which case wake me up before you go. I have a few things for the two of you that may be of help to you."

"You don't think that's going to happen, do you? I mean, surely she would keep us close so Dez can help protect her."

"Who can say?" Grandma asked. "There may yet be things for you to discover outside the palace walls. Queen Maivelynn will determine that during your audience with her."

"Oh, I haven't told Dez about that yet."

Grandma smiled and patted Allie's hand. "I'm sure the queen saw to it that he was informed, but if it will make you feel better I will tell him on my way out."

"Would you please?" Allie asked.

"Certainly," Grandma said. "Enjoy the rest of your meal. I'll see you in the morning, if not later this evening."

As Grandma left the dining hall, Lord Drake approached Allie's table where she now sat alone. "I'm a little surprised to see you here this evening," he began. "Anything wrong?"

Allie shook her head. "Not necessarily. Just wanted to update the queen on what we've learned so far."

Drake raised an eyebrow. "Anything I should know about."

Shrugging, Allie replied, "I suppose if Queen Maivelynn sees the need to inform you and the rest of the council, she will. I think it would be wisest for me not to say anything else until I've spoken with her."

"I see," Drake said slowly. "I've heard rumors that someone on the council is involved."

Allie looked at him. She was once again struck by the differences between Drake and her father. Where it was always easy to tell what her father was thinking, Drake was unreadable. She chose her words carefully. "I believe you'll find that's merely idle gossip. Nothing in our investigation has given us any reason to believe a Fey Council member is part of what's going on."

"That's good to hear." Drake smiled. "I am glad to see you

again, Allie. Perhaps after you see more of the Fey Realm, you'll choose to stay here indefinitely."

"I really can't see that happening until after I finish school, Uncle Drake. But I will keep it mind," she added when a frown replaced his smile.

He bowed. "Can't ask for more than that, I suppose. Have a good evening and if there's anything you would like to discuss with me, you are always welcome to visit."

"Thank you." Allie watched Drake wander about the dining hall, stopping at tables to talk to people he knew before he disappeared out the doors. She sighed, left alone once again, and looked around. She could see Maivelynn and Nightwind meandering the garden. The queen looked so calm, as though there wasn't a thing in the world to be worried about. Allie envied her. She wished she felt calm. Her stomach was a knot of nerves and her brain wouldn't stop spinning through various situations, each worse than the one before it. She jumped as a hand touched her shoulder.

"Sorry to startle you," Dez said with his quirky grin. "I thought perhaps you'd like to walk out in the garden before we visit with the queen. You look like you could release some pent-up energy."

Allie smiled at him. "I'd like that."

He held her chair while she rose from her seat before leading her out the courtyard doors. They were quiet for a few moments as they walked underneath the trees. The sun was setting in a glorious display of colors. Allie had never seen anything so beautiful, and yet her mind wouldn't be still. After a while, Dez said, "Tell me what you're thinking about, Allie."

"Oh, everything and nothing," she replied. "The things we've heard today, everything I've learned in less than forty-eight hours." Allie sighed. "It's all a bit overwhelming."

Dez nodded. "I can understand that. Perhaps not to the extent you're feeling it, but I do understand that feeling of being lost."

Allie glanced at him. "Grandma and Lord Drake have both said you've been my guardian for a long time. How old are you?"

He chuckled, "Isn't that on the no-no list of questions to ask?"

"Only if you're asking a lady," she retorted.

"Men don't get to hide their age, huh?"

She shook her head with a grin. "Nope."

"So unfair," Dez replied with mock hurt. "In all honesty, I'm not much older than you are."

"Meaning?" Allie pressed.

"I'm twenty-six," he admitted. "So, truly, not that much older than you are."

"And you're a real twenty-six, not some kind of weird Fey calendar twenty-six?"

Dez laughed. "The Fey calendar is the same as the mortal one, so yes I'm a real twenty-six. No extra zeroes for you to worry about. Why?"

She blushed. "Just curious. I mean, being a guardian seems like it would be an important job. Something for people who are, you know, older and more experienced."

"It is an important job," he said, stopping for a moment. "Being guardian of the Fey Princess is especially important. And you're right. Normally it is a job for older, more experienced guardians."

"How did you get that job so young?"

Dez looked away from her, pain flickering in his eyes. "I've had experiences most around here have not."

Allie put a hand on his uninjured arm. "I'm sorry, Dez. You don't have to tell me about it, if you don't want to."

He laid his hand over hers with a smile. "Thanks, Allie. Some days are better than others and perhaps someday I'll tell you about it. But not today. The reality is, I'm glad I'm your guardian. You're going to be a great queen someday."

"You think so?"

Dez kissed her forehead. "I know so." He blushed. "Sorry, I shouldn't have done that."

Allie smiled. "I didn't mind." To be honest, she'd rather enjoyed it. Warmth spread throughout her from the simple gesture. She suddenly hoped this part of the garden wasn't visible from the suite she and her grandmother shared. Otherwise she'd never be able to keep her growing feelings for her fairy guardian to herself.

Chapter 21

The queen's chambers were lavishly decorated. Allie looked about herself in awe at crystal chandeliers, a large fireplace, and lush carpets in a mossy green. Leaf and vine motifs were found throughout the room both on the furnishings and the walls. One wall boasted a lovely painting of a summer meadow. Allie could almost imagine the flowers nodding in an unseen breeze. She turned her attention to Maivelynn as the queen entered the room, Lord Nightwind at her side. Allie curtsied as Dez bowed low.

"Welcome, friends," Maivelynn said with a smile. "Shall I have some tea or chocolate served?"

Remembering the creamy hot chocolate Grandma had

somehow procured, Allie replied, "Hot chocolate sounds good, if that's all right."

Maivelynn laughed. "It is absolutely all right. Between the three of us, I've always preferred a good pot of chocolate to tea. Just something soothing about it, wouldn't you say?" She nodded to a servant standing nearby and the servant disappeared out the door with a bow. "Now, let's talk about why you desired this audience with me, Allie." She motioned for them to be seated while Nightwind took his place lying next to her on the carpet. "I suppose you aren't here with good news."

"I'm afraid not, my queen," Dez admitted. "We learned much today and what we learned leads us to believe the attack on Allie was a ruse."

The servant returned with a tray laden with a gleaming silver pot, three mugs, and a plate of cookies and scones. "Thank you, Calliope," Maivelynn said to her before turning her attention back to Dez. She served mugs of chocolate to everyone before asking, "A ruse? In what way?"

Dez related the information they'd learned at Cynthia's apartment as well as what they'd heard at The Green Villain. "Twyla was not being fully honest with me, nothing I could charge her with, of course," he added with a scowl, "but enough missing pieces to make her information almost useless."

"The list of ingredients she gave you, what all was on it?" Maivelynn asked.

"All the normal things you would expect in a sleeping potion except for one. This potion, if we can trust her, had dragonbane extract in it."

Nightwind snorted as his head jerked up. "Dragonbane? That can be lethal if not used properly."

"Yes, which is why Twyla joked the person it was used against should still be sleeping," Dez replied. "However, dragonbane extract and essence of nightshade typically counteract one another. If done correctly, this potion would essentially be rendered useless. It would knock Allie out for a few moments, which is what happened, but she would have woken soon enough to fight against her attackers, assuming I was not quick enough to save her myself."

Maivelynn frowned. "This is deeply troubling. What purpose would an attempted kidnapping serve?"

"Well, it frightened the crud out of me," Allie admitted. "And it drew attention away from the realm, and more importantly you."

"You think the person behind this is actually interested in

me?"

Dez sighed, "Everything points that way, Your Majesty. From what Cynthia told us, there are still some in the Hollow who feel they are not treated as equally as others. They feel looked down upon."

Maivelynn ran an exasperated hand over Nightwind's neck. "That's ridiculous. Nyx hasn't been queen in over four hundred years. I'll admit there was a long time of suspicion around them, it makes sense that there would be. Elves were once seen in a poor light too after the whole Erlkönig business."

"That German poem?" Allie asked.

"Based, loosely, on a dark elf who called himself the Elf King, or Erlkönig in German," Maivelynn explained. "He would have been a great healer, if he didn't prefer spreading the diseases he could prevent. He wreaked havoc on eastern Europe, but most especially in Germany where he felt slighted in some way. I honestly can't remember the reason for his anger with them. There's a reason superstition and fear still surround the Black Forest."

"Mermaids have been looked sourly upon, as well as every other Fey group," Dez added.

"Even unicorns have shared their time in the unwanted

spotlight," Nightwind said. "I wonder though, my queen, if there is still lingering suspicion around the witch community simply because Nyx wasn't just some rogue member, but Queen of the Fey. That makes her far more powerful, and dangerous, than your typical Fey."

Maivelynn paused with a frown. "I suppose there could be residual doubts. And of course, there could also be perceived doubts which in reality are unfounded." She sighed. "Well, this is not at all what I expected to learn from this investigation. It bothers me deeply that someone would wish to make members of the Fey Council appear untrustworthy, especially Hazel. It is no secret that she and I have been friends for many, many years. An effort to undermine her authority within the council could be disastrous."

"What about Xylia, the other witch on the Fey Council Cynthia mentioned?" Allie asked.

"I'm not very close to Xylia," Maivelynn admitted. "She's a quiet sort, but I wouldn't fear any rebellion from her. She's as gentle as a spring rain."

Allie found the description odd since where she was from spring rains were rarely gentle, but she kept the thought to herself. "What should we do?"

Maivelynn didn't respond right away, her hand stroking

Nightwind's neck as she thought. "We proceed as though you hadn't discovered this."

"What?" Dez demanded. "My queen, your safety! The Realm!"

"At the moment, Dezydery, the only ones who know of this are in this room, and I would assume Allie's grandmother. How would it look if suddenly my security was doubled? Or you called off your investigation without actually discovering the culprit?" She paused to allow this to sink in. "If we proceed as though this conversation never took place, we have the upper hand. The person or persons behind this plot will believe their plan is going according to their desires."

"But, Queen Maivelynn, if they attack before we return at the end of the appointed time for our investigation, you'll need us," Allie said.

"Actually, I'll need you far away. There is something neither of you have considered. At any given time, there is only one Queen of the Fey and only one Princess of the Fey. In this way we avoid the succession problems which have plagued mortals so often. If there's only one princess, then there is no question who becomes queen when the time comes. However, there is a downfall to this set up. Because there is only one Princess of the Fey, if something happens to

163

the queen and the princess is unable to take her place, whether because she is too young or she also has been removed in some way, that leaves the Fey Realm with no clear successor." She looked at Dez seriously. "You know enough of our history to know how terrible that can be."

Dez nodded with a frown. "I still don't like this idea, Queen Maivelynn. It leaves you vulnerable."

She smiled. "I'm not vulnerable as long as I have Lord Nightwind at my side. He has kept constant guard over me for many years and proved himself against many foes. I'd rather have him at my side than a thousand royal guardians."

The unicorn ducked his head. "You're making me blush."

Maivelynn laughed. "Like anyone could tell with your dark coat." She turned once more to Allie and Dez. "I wish you to continue your investigation. Find out who was behind the attempted kidnapping. If you can discover that, you can find out who is behind the larger plot. Stay in the palace for the night, but leave early tomorrow. At this point, many of the council will have seen you at supper. Let's have them assume you merely stopped in for the night."

Dez stood and Allie hesitated for a moment. "Queen Maivelynn, if something does happen, what should we do?"

The queen smiled, though it lacked its normal summer

warmth. "Take care of the Fey Realm, of course. Good night."

Chapter 22

Dez walked Allie to her suite, pausing momentarily for Lady Xylia to pass them in the hall. When they arrived, he paused again and, for the first time Allie had seen, looked uncomfortable. "Mind if I come in for a little while?" he asked.

"Not at all," Allie said. "I'd appreciate the company."

"Thanks."

They entered the suite and Allie sat down by the open parlor windows. The buttery yellow moon peeked over the tree line. Night flowers bloomed, releasing their perfume into the chill autumn air. Allie wrapped her arms around herself. She glanced at Dez, who still appeared ill at ease as he paced the room. "Something's bothering you. What is it?"

"I don't like leaving Queen Maivelynn unprotected," he growled.

"She's not unprotected, "Allie pointed out, keeping her tone gentle, though she shared Dez's frustration. "She has her own guardians and she has Lord Nightwind with her. He would never allow her to come to harm."

"Not if he could prevent it, no," Dez agreed reluctantly. He ran his hands through his hair, letting them come to a stop on his shoulders. He looked at Allie. "You think I worry too much, don't you?"

Allie smirked. "Well, maybe a little." When he didn't smile, she sighed. "Dez, this is all so new to me. But I think you take your responsibilities very seriously. Perhaps too seriously. Maybe Queen Maivelynn is right. Maybe if we continue as though we didn't know about the plot, we will have the upper hand."

"Not in my experience," Dez replied in a whisper, leaning on the windowsill and looking out away from her.

Unsure how to comfort him, she stood and moved closer to him, placing a gentle hand on his arm. "I don't know what your experience has been, but we need to trust the queen. Right? Isn't that what you would tell me if I were the one questioning how to proceed?"

Dez shook his head. "A good guardian trusts no one. He trusts his instincts."

She took a moment to observe him. The stubborn set of his jaw, the moonlight highlighting his hair. An unearthly glow lit his honey-colored eyes, similar to when he'd prepared to hold back the dragon. "What do your instincts tell you now?"

"We should stay," he said quietly. "Queen Maivelynn needs all the help she can get. We'll make it look like we're continuing the investigation, but we stay close to the palace."

Allie nodded. "Okay."

He looked at her for a moment, question in his eyes. "You're not going to argue with me?"

Shaking her head, Allie said, "Not this time. I'm not a guardian. I'm not even sure how good a princess I am," she added with a small laugh. "But I'm also not you. You are a guardian, and I trust you. If you think we should stay close to the palace, then that's what we'll do."

The right corner of his mouth quirked into a grin. "I knew I liked you for a reason."

She blushed with a laugh. "Glad I could keep you happy."

Their conversation was interrupted by the sound of twigs snapping outside. Dez immediately turned to the window, using his arm to guide Allie behind himself. "Get down and stay down," he whispered.

Allie ducked down and crawled to the wall where she could watch Dez, but stay hidden from anyone outside. His eyes searched for the source of the noise and a faint glow appeared around him. Without warning, he hopped over the edge of the windowsill. Her voice strained from trying to stay quiet, Allie called, "Dez!" She peeked over the edge of the windowsill as Dez disappeared into the trees. For a moment, she hesitated. Dez would probably tell her to stay where she was. But not knowing if he was safe gnawed at her. Making her decision, she jumped out the open window. It was close to the ground, so the impact wasn't as jarring as it could have been. She took a moment to get her bearings before running in the direction Dez had gone. The trees were closer together than she'd realized. She battled her way between thorny bushes and gnarled trees, getting turned around more times than she could count. In moments, she was hopelessly lost. Pausing to catch her breath, Allie's eyes darted around. "How can I find Dez if I don't even know where I am?"

"Whither do you go?"

Looking around herself and seeing no one, Allie asked, "Who is that?"

"I am called Artemios, my princess. Whither do you go?"

Still unable to find the speaker, she hesitated. Dez told her that a good guardian trusted no one and she believed that meant she shouldn't give her trust too easily either. Certainly that included disembodied voices.

"I cannot help if you give no answer."

"Where are you?" she demanded.

The voice chuckled. "Look up."

Allie glanced up. A glowing bird, the size of a small falcon sat on a high branch in a tree watching her. "A hercinia?" she asked in wonder.

"It pleases me to know we are not entirely forgotten by the world," the bird replied, flying down and landing on a closer branch. "So few of us remain. But please, my name is Artemios and I would be most pleased if you called me by it."

"Okay," Allie said slowly. She tried to think back to the medieval legends her parents had taught her. Could hercinias speak? She couldn't remember. Of course, did it really matter what the legends said? Artemios looked exactly as she'd always pictured the benevolent bird. His dark, round eyes were kind as he observed her. A silvery glow, soft as moonlight, emanated from his feathers. Perhaps she should trust him. She'd never heard of a hercinia leading anyone astray.

"How can I be of assistance, Your Highness?" he asked.

"First, just call me Allie, and second, I'm trying to find my guardian. He ran into the woods a while ago and I haven't been able to find him."

Artemios bobbed his head. "It is easy to become lost in these woods, but have no fear. We will find your missing guardian." He spread his wings and shook them, a single feather falling to the ground. "Ah, your guardian is north of here," he said, looking at where the tip of the feather pointed. "Come, Allie." The hercinia lifted from the branch and flew away. Allie jogged to keep up with the bird, while at the same time trying to keep an eye on the ground. After a while he dropped another feather and they turned east. "There, my princess." Her guardian lay motionless on the ground.

"Dez!" she cried, running to his side. His fairy countenance flickered and she saw tears in his wings. "Oh, Dez, can you hear me?"

"I will request help from the castle," Artemios said, flying into the air.

Allie nodded and turned back to Dez. "Please, wake up."

"I am awake," he groaned, barely opening his eyes to look at her. "I wish I weren't."

"What can I do to help?" she asked.

"Not much, unfortunately, unless you happen to be a Healer like your grandmother," Dez replied, struggling to sit up.

Allie pushed him back. "You should stay still until someone has a chance to look at you. Who did this?"

Dez sighed. "Our friend. Only, he wasn't alone." He eyed Allie for a moment. "Who were you talking to earlier?"

"When?"

"What do you mean when?" Dez repeated with a snort. "When you thought I couldn't hear you."

"Oh, just a hercinia named Artemios." She noticed the hard line of his mouth. "Why?"

He grimaced. "Just wanted to make sure you were safe. Not that I could do much right now to keep you that way." He shifted again and groaned.

"Lie still."

"Easy for you to say," Dez grunted. "You're not the one lying on rocks."

Allie chuckled and shook her head. She shifted around. "Here, put your head in my lap, that will at least be somewhat more comfortable."

"It wouldn't be appropriate," he replied, looking away

from her.

Snorting, she retorted, "Who cares?" She lifted his head gently and placed it in her lap. Unable to stop herself, she ran her fingers through the silky strands of his hair. He winced as she found a large knot on the side of his head. "Good golly! What did you get hit with, a brick?"

"Club, but it had the same effect."

"Dez, Allie," Grandma said as she came behind Artemios. "What happened?"

"The dark elf we saw earlier ambushed me with a rather vicious troll on his side," Dez replied.

Grandma clucked her tongue as she looked Dez over. "Wasn't a dragon enough for one day, young man?"

He smiled, though it quickly became a grimace as Grandma worked. "I guess not." Suddenly he looked over at Allie. "What are you doing out here anyway? I told you to stay put."

"I wasn't going to let you just run off into the woods on your own," she snapped. "Besides, it's a good thing I followed you. You might have died out here."

"I would have made it back to the castle just fine on my own," Dez retorted.

"Ha, that's what you think," Grandma replied. "You won't

be flying anywhere for a long while and you've got a broken leg. What would you have done? Crawled to the palace?"

"If that's what it took," he scowled.

Allie glared at him. "Why are you being so surly all of a sudden?"

"Because his pride is hurt," Grandma muttered, splinting Dez's leg with a stick Artemios brought her.

"Because it's my job to keep Allie safe" he spat. "Going into any forest after nightfall is dangerous, especially with a dark elf and a troll in cahoots with each other."

At any other time, Allie would have laughed at the old-fashioned word. But right now anger filled her. "I came out here to help you and to make sure you were all right. And it's a good thing I did or you might have died or caused yourself worse injury. I'm not a baby, Dez, I can take care of myself."

He snorted. "Oh really?"

"Yes, really."

"Stop," Grandma said, covering Dez's mouth with her hand. "The two of you will stop this instant. You need each other and right now, Dez, Allie is right. It's a good thing she came out to find you. And having Artemios help her ensured you got the help you needed. Allie, Dez has a point too. You are very new to this world and don't fully know or understand its dangers."

"And who's fault is that?" Allie snapped, angry tears filling her eyes as she stood. "I don't know what I need to because you and Dad and Mom spent my whole life lying to me. So if I'm ignorant, you have no one to blame but yourself."

"Allie…"

But Allie didn't hear what her grandmother had to say. She was already running back toward the castle.

Chapter 23

It didn't take as long to reach the castle as she would have expected. Once inside her suite, Allie slammed the door of her room shut and let herself collapse against it. Her sides ached and her breathing came in painful gasps. She swiped at the tears rolling down her cheeks. "Some princess I am," she muttered.

"You are an excellent princess," a voice came from the window.

Allie glanced over in surprise. "Artemios?"

"I pray you won't find my following you too presumptuous," the hercinia replied from the windowsill. "I wanted only to ensure you arrived safely home."

She wiped at her face again. "I don't mind, Artemios. Thanks."

"May I enter?" he asked.

Allie nodded, not sure she trusted her voice. She watched the glowing bird flutter from the windowsill to one of the posts on her bed.

"What has my princess so incensed?" Artemios asked when they sat in silence for several moments.

Swiping again at her tears, Allie groaned. "Everything."

Artemios chuckled. "It cannot be everything, Allie. Surely I have not earned your anger."

She gave a weak laugh. "Ugh, no. But this whole situation is completely beyond my control. No one asked if I wanted to be a princess. No one told me anything about this place. Up until yesterday, I would have thought you were just a fictional character in stories written by superstitious dreamers. And now I'm stuck in a world I don't understand, trying to save it from an evil I can't comprehend, and," her voice broke as fresh tears spilled past her eyelashes, "I'm scared."

He fluttered down next to her. "There is no shame in being afraid, Allie. Even the most courageous of heroes feel fear."

Allie rolled her eyes. "That's what everyone says. It doesn't make it any easier to accept."

Chuckling again, Artemios said, "No, I suppose not. You just said yesterday you would have believed me to be a myth, something created from an overzealous imagination."

"Sorry," Allie murmured.

"Do not apologize for what is true. I suppose most of humanity believes I am just a myth, if they've heard of me at all. If you told anyone you had a luminescent bird as a companion, they would mock you. 'Surely such things are the product of the mind,' they would say," Artemios explained. "Imagine if you believed them. Where would that leave me? Many of the lesser-known Fey creatures are disappearing from the world. Too few believe in us anymore. We're not like dragons and unicorns and mermaids, which every young child hopes and believes to be real somewhere. As the world forgets us, we fade from existence. That is what I fear, Allie. I fear being forgotten to the point of fading entirely from human memory." He glanced up at her, his dark eyes reflecting the lantern light of her room. "Your very presence here has helped both of us. You have learned your true identity as the future queen of our land. And I have gained a much-needed friend and hope that perhaps I will not be forgotten as I fear."

"But there's still so much I don't know."

Artemios seemed to smile as he replied, "Then I and your guardian shall help you learn. I cannot say why you did not know of our world before, and it is not my place to ask. However, I can help you learn all you need to know to become the princess, nay, the queen I know resides in your heart."

"How can you be so sure?"

"Some things are just known, dear Allie," Artemios replied, brushing her knee with his wing.

A smile lit Allie's face. "Thank you, Artemios."

He bobbed his head. "I shall return in the morning. For now, get some rest. Your grandmother will be able to help Dez back to the castle. I'm sure by now his leg is healed."

"What about his wings?" Allie asked. "They were torn."

Artemios turned to her. There was a frown in his voice as he replied, "I do not know, Your Highness. Fairy wings are delicate like a butterfly's wings. Depending on how powerful your grandmother is, she may or may not be able to heal the damage inflicted."

She frowned. "Maybe I should wait for them in the parlor."

"Nay, my princess. You need rest. I shall wait for them and you can see how he is healing tomorrow. For now, sleep. Be at ease."

"Artemios?"

"Yes, Allie?"

"Why do you speak the way you do? You sound very," she hesitated, not wanting to offend the one being who wasn't treating her like a fragile child, "formal, like you're from a different time."

The hercinia chuckled. "One might say that I am from a different time, Your Highness. Sleep well." Artemios lifted up and flew out the open window, his wings aglow with moonlight and the magic that made him so unique.

Allie changed for bed and lay down on the downy mattress. She heard her grandmother enter the suite. Part of her wanted to go apologize for her outburst, but bitterness still clung to her. Deciding there would be time to talk in the morning, she closed her eyes and tried to take Artemios' advice. Within moments, she fell into a deep sleep.

~*~

The wind picked up sometime during the night and Allie woke up feeling chilled. The gauzy curtains fluttered. Allie got out of bed, wrapping her robe tightly around herself. She walked to the window and looked around for a way to block the chill breeze. She wondered briefly how anyone could stand the rooms during the winter. While the Summer Wood was enchanting and beautiful, it apparently still experienced the same weather as the rest of the world. Was there some magic spell that would allow her to put a pane of glass between herself and the elements? If there was, she certainly didn't know it. Not finding an immediate solution to her problem, Allie pulled the robe tighter and wandered through the room hoping to find an extra blanket to add to her bed. She glanced through the tall wardrobe and in the closet, not finding anything. Her teeth began chattering as the air grew colder. She glanced at the window. Snowflakes fluttered past. A frown tugged at Allie's lips. While it wasn't unheard of for snow to fall in October, it usually didn't fall this early. She began walking toward the window, but startled as a glowing bird flew in. "Artemios?"

"Hush, Allie," he said, his voice urgent. "Stay away from the window. Follow me." He led her deeper into the room and into a corner of the closet after she picked up the stone Cynthia had given her. He shook out his wings and a feather fell, the tip pointing to the back wall. He began searching it before pressing his beak against a small symbol. The wall opened up. "Pick up the feather and follow me. Pray, make no noise and stay close to me. My luminescence is dimmed when I'm not outside in the natural light of the world."

Allie picked up the glowing feather, marveling at its softness before following Artemios into the hidden passage. A million questions zipped through her mind, but she kept quiet. Artemios led her down a narrow hallway, his glow fading as they continued. She stopped abruptly as they reached a dead end.

"Wait here, I shall go ahead and be sure we are safe," Artemios said.

"Where are we?" Allie whispered.

"We are at the quarters of the guardians," he replied. "Before you go rushing in, I must see that your guardian is sufficiently healed to take you to safety. If not, I shall do the best I can to lead you to a new haven."

"I thought Summer Wood was supposed to be safe." Allie heard the whimper in her own voice and wished she could banish it. Now was not the time to be afraid. It was time to be strong.

Artemios sighed. "Alas, my princess, I fear those days are behind us. One can only hope it will be a temporary change. Now, please, wait here." He pushed a symbol on the wall and it opened up to him. He flew into the room and as the wall slid shut once again, Allie hoped he wouldn't be gone long.

Chapter 24

The seconds crawled by as Allie waited for Artemios to return. She wondered if the thunderous beating of her heart could be heard echoing through the dark tunnel. Even her breathing sounded loud as she pressed against the wall. The scraping sound of the hidden door opening caught Allie's attention as lantern light illuminated the tunnel. "Allie, come on in," Dez said, his voice gruff. Dark circles shadowed his eyes and his hair stood out at odd angles.

"Sorry to wake you up, I'm sure it's nothing..."

"Never assume it's nothing, Allie," Dez replied. "I'm glad Artemios brought you. Give me a minute to pack a few things and then we'll head out."

"Wait, should I have packed something?" Allie asked.

Dez shrugged with a yawn. "Maybe, but it's too late now. You can't go back to your room."

"Well, Artemios could just lead me back down the tunnel," she said.

Shaking his head, Dez sighed. "Allie, this has nothing to do with your ability to get back to your room and everything to do with if it's safe to go back to your room. Trust me, it's not safe for you to go back."

Allie paled. "What about Grandma? She's still in the suite. What if someone hurts her?"

"Your grandmother will be fine," Artemios said in a gentle tone.

Dez nodded. "They're not interested in her. They want you. I've got some theories as to what our unknown enemy wants. If you and I, especially you, are already gone in the morning, our suspect just might think their plan in working. Unless of course they're handling things themselves, in which case they won't be fooled. But I highly doubt it."

"What's your theory?" she asked.

"We'll discuss it later. For now, have a seat while I gather some things," he said, pointing out a plain wooden chair.

"Okay." Allie glanced around the room. Where her suite

was richly decorated, the guardians' quarters were plain and simple. She supposed it made sense. The guardians probably didn't spend much time here.

Dez continued speaking which pulled her attention back to him. "This is not going to be an easy journey, but I'll do what I can to make it safe for you."

He walked away and Allie noticed he was limping. She frowned. "Is he going to be able to do this?" she asked Artemios in a whisper.

The hercinia chuckled. "Whether or not it would be wise, he will do it anyway. Your guardian is quite determined."

"Stubborn would be a better word for Dez," Allie muttered.

Artemios laughed. "Mayhap it would."

"No more stubborn than you," Dez said, coming into the room with a bag slung over his shoulder. "All right, follow me and be extremely quiet. In order for our ruse to work, we need everyone in the castle to believe you've been carried off."

"Wait, shouldn't we let my grandmother know I'm safe? She'll worry," Allie pointed out.

"All the more reason to not leave a message. We need to make it appear that you've been taken, Allie. It's the best way for us to uncover the truth," Dez explained. "Besides, if I know anything at all about your grandma, it's that she can handle herself and anything thrown at her."

"Maybe," Allie said slowly. "I still don't like leaving without letting her know I'm safe. We didn't exactly part on friendly terms last night."

"I don't think you parted with anyone on friendly terms last night," Dez retorted.

"Untrue. The princess and I had a very pleasant chat yestereve," Artemios countered.

Dez rolled his eyes. "Well, at least you weren't snapping at everyone. Now we need to go, before we wake the other guardians. Many of us are light sleepers." He opened the door to the hallway and glanced around outside before motioning for Allie and Artemios to follow him. They walked on silent feet down the hall and turned down a dimly lit corridor. Dez pulled on a bronze lamp and a wall opened up next to it. He held a finger to his lips and led them into the dark. Once the wall closed behind them, Dez struck a match and lit a small lantern. "If you must speak, do so in a whisper," he said, "at least until we reach outside. This tunnel isn't as well-known as some of the other passages in the castle, but we don't want to draw unwanted attention to our escape."

"Do you really think Grandma will be all right?" Allie asked, her uncertainty making her quiver.

Dez took her hand and squeezed it. "I'm sure she'll be fine."

The warmth and strength in his touch calmed her as Allie followed him through the underground tunnel. Artemios flew around them, sometimes ahead and sometimes behind. Allie shivered as the cool air surrounded them. Dez stopped and hung the lantern on a nearby hook in the wall. He pulled something out of his bag. "Here. This will keep you warmer than your robe will."

"What is it?" she asked as Dez patiently waited for her to shed her robe.

"A winter cloak. And don't worry, I brought two." He adjusted the cloak over Allie's shoulders and helped her clasp the dragonfly-shaped closure. When finished, he looked up at her. For a moment, Allie just stared into his honey-brown eyes mesmerized by the swirl of emotions she saw there. He brushed a stray wisp of hair away from her face, his hand lingering on her cheek. Then he turned away and picked up the lantern. "We should keep going."

They walked in silence for several minutes. Allie's thoughts tumbled over each other as they continued along the tunnel. It had widened out and Allie realized it was probably part of the underground cavern she'd been in earlier. "Do you learn about all the passages as part of being a guardian?"

"Not all of them," Dez replied with a shrug. "It's dangerous for anyone to know every passageway, but each guardian knows a handful. The only person who knows about all of them is the queen. That's how it's always been."

"How does she learn about them?"

Dez smiled. "When she became queen, Maivelynn was taken in turn by each of the guardians at the time to inspect the passageways they knew about. In doing this, she was able to learn every passage, giving her multiple means of escape in case she needed it. It has always been done that way. When you become queen, you will be taken through the castle just as the queens before you were. Here we are." He stopped in front of a tangle of tree roots.

"Shall I go first to be certain no one awaits us?" Artemios asked.

"I think that would be wise," Dez replied.

The bird bobbed his head and as soon as Dez opened the passage, he flew out. Dez stood in the newly found doorway waiting for Artemios to return. When he did, Artemios said, "All is well."

"Let's go then." Dez took Allie's hand again and led her out of the cavern.

Chapter 25

Filtered sunlight woke Allie as the leaves rustled in a chill breeze above her. She groaned as she sat up. Instead of her soft mattress, she was lying on the cold, hard ground. Memories stirred in her as her mind slowly came back into reality. Dez had led her deep into the woods during the night until they were both too exhausted to go on. He'd made a rudimentary camp and insisted she get some sleep. As she looked around, she saw Dez sat on a small log poking at a fire. Artemios slept peacefully on a tree branch above them. If memory served, Dez was building that fire when she went to sleep.

"Sleep well, princess?" Dez asked as she came closer.

"Well enough for sleeping in the snow," she replied with a small shiver. "What about you?"

Dez shrugged.

"You know that's not an actual answer, right?" Allie said. She took in the dark shadows under his eyes and his pale complexion. "You didn't sleep at all last night did you?"

He rubbed a hand across the stubble growing on his chin. "Not since Artemios woke me. And truth be told, I didn't sleep well before that either."

"Why not?"

"I think you know why."

Allie blinked. "I'm not sure why I would."

He ran a frustrated hand through his hair. "You weren't the only one being snappish yesterday, Allie. It wasn't fair of me to get mad at you. In your shoes, I would have done exactly the same thing. What you did was stupid, make no mistake," he added, pointing his stick at her. "And you need to learn to follow my directions. But it was brave too and it probably did save my life. So, I'm sorry for being a jerk. And thank you."

She smiled. "You're forgiven and you're welcome." A biting wind blew through the glade and Allie pulled the cloak tighter about herself. "Ugh, I wish I had my boots right now."

"Slippers probably don't help much in the snow, do they?"

Dez asked.

Allie shook her head. "Not particularly."

"We can probably risk a trip to your apartment to get a few more essentials. Somehow I don't think that nightgown of yours is very warm either."

Warmth flooded her cheeks as the realization that she was still in pajamas hit her. "Yeah, not much."

He chuckled. "Then we'll definitely make a stop at your apartment. Perhaps we'll stop in on Mrs. Lampwick again for more cookies. I was disappointed when we lost the last of them."

"I'm sure she'd love the visit." They were quiet for a moment and Allie asked, "Dez, why have I never seen myself as an elf? I mean, you say you can see me as I am. But I can't."

Shrugging, he said, "Probably because you're not looking to see yourself as an elf."

"Huh?"

"It's kind of like the difference of what people see in you and what you see when you look in a mirror. I could tell you that you have eyes the exact shade as perfect aquamarines, your hair looks sleek and beautiful even after sleeping on the ground, and you have a smile that could light up the darkest day. But I bet if I handed you a mirror, you wouldn't see that. You would see the bags under your eyes from not sleeping enough, the few stray hairs which aren't exactly in the right place, and any blemishes you think you might have. I would guess that when you've passed by a mirror in the time since discovering your true identity, you've been looking at who you think you are. You're not seeing yourself as you really are."

"So, how do I see myself the way you see me?"

Gold flecks danced in his eyes as Dez looked at her and said gently, "You have to believe yourself to be what I say you are. If you believed yourself to be the beautiful elf I see, you would see her too." He paused for a moment, watching her. "You can move closer to the fire if you need to. Your face is pink."

Allie wanted to look away from him, knowing the pink in her cheeks had nothing to do with the cold. But at the same time, she couldn't. Dez was unlike anyone she'd ever met, and not just because he had hidden wings and a knack for showing up just when she needed him. He was able to irritate and annoy her past the point of rational thought and then turn around and say something so tender and sweet that her heart melted into a puddle of sentiment.

His lips quirked into a half-grin, as though he knew what she'd been thinking. "I guess since we're both awake, we should probably make some breakfast."

"Anything I can do to help?" Allie asked, wishing she could make the burning in her cheeks stop.

"Nah, I've got this."

Allie sat quietly watching him work before going back to where she'd been sleeping. The small bedroll Dez had given her should probably be put away. She rolled it up, thinking of the night before. Walking through the forest in the moonlight might have been romantic, had it not been for the bitter cold and the eerie sense of danger following them. She wasn't sure how long they walked, sometimes backtracking and taking random turns. Every now and again, Artemios would swoop close to Dez and in hushed whispers tell him what he'd seen ahead of them. By the time they reached the little glade, Allie was cold, miserable, and exhausted. Dez had set things up for her so she could rest, apologizing for not having more available for her. Despite the ground being hard, she'd fallen asleep quickly. Now as she carried the makeshift bedding over to Dez, she wished she'd stayed up long enough to remind her guardian that he needed rest too. "I'm not sure where exactly this goes," she said as she stopped in front of him.

He took the bedroll from her and tied it to the outside of his bag. "Thanks. You did a good job rolling it up."

Allie shrugged. "My family goes camping at least once a year, more often when Dad's not too busy."

"What does your dad do?"

"He works with real estate, fixing up older homes and making them beautiful again. He loves it and it gives him a chance to be creative like Mom, just in a different way."

"Your mom is an artist."

Allie nodded. "Yeah."

"So how is it you're going into such an uncreative field?" Dez asked. "I mean, I would think with both of your parents having a form of artistry about them, maybe you would too."

"I don't know," she replied. "I mean, I've always liked animals and wanted to help them. Being an artist or fixing up houses isn't going to help anyone's pet get better."

Dez smiled. "I think you'll be good at it. And now, breakfast is served. It's not much, but it should keep us going for the day."

He handed her a tin plate with oatmeal and dried berries. Then he motioned to the pot of boiled water and held up a few small packets. "There's enough to make cocoa. Won't be nearly as good as the chocolate Queen Maivelynn has."

"Cocoa from a packet is never as good as homemade," Allie said. "But I can think of worse things to have to drink."

Dez chuckled. "I'm sure you can." He mixed a packet into a camp mug of water. "Enjoy."

They were quiet a moment as they began eating and Allie glanced up at Artemios. "Will he wake up anytime soon?"

"Probably not," Dez replied. "Hercinias are typically nocturnal anyway and he had a long night last night. But he'll know how to find you. Don't worry about him. For today, we're going to worry about keeping you safe and continuing our investigation."

"What if you get hurt again?" Allie asked.

He sighed and looked at her. "Allie, yesterday I was stupid. I shouldn't have chased him into the woods without backup. And while you're certainly brave and stubborn, you're really not the kind of person who can give good backup."

"Not really," she admitted.

"I don't think another attack like that will happen today. For as bad as I looked yesterday, I gave as good as I got. That troll is no longer a threat."

"And the elf?"

Dez scowled. "He got away. Again." He smacked his fist into his other hand. "I've never had a suspect elude me twice."

"I'm sorry."

"No, I should be sorry. Catching him could be the key to finding out what is going on." He sighed. "I guess next time, right?"

"Sure." Silence fell over them until Allie asked, "Dez, why can't I see you as a fairy even when I focus? The only times I've seen you in fairy mode is when you've been using your skills."

"Fairy mode?" he teased.

"Hey, I don't know what to call it," she retorted. "But seriously, why?"

He laughed, though without mirth. "Bad habit. I'm so used to hiding my identity, I very rarely allow my guard down enough for people to recognize what I am. There are even some of the other guardians who have never seen me, and we train to see everything for what it is."

"Why?"

Dez shook his head. "Not now, Allie. You finished?"

She handed him her empty plate and mug. As he rinsed them with the leftover water from their breakfast, she asked the final question which had plagued her through the night. "Dez, has there ever been a King of the Fey?"

For a long moment, Dez didn't respond. "Why do you

ask?"

"I've seen all the statues of the queens, but never any kings. Are queens required to stay single or something?"

"There has never been a king, not in the sense mortals use the word," Dez said slowly, refusing to look at her. "The Fey have always been led by a female."

"But the queen doesn't have to be single, does she?" Allie asked, desperate for a straight answer.

Dez looked at her, his eyes searching hers. After a moment, he smiled. "No, Allie, the queen doesn't have to stay single. Many have had romantic relationships and some even married and had families. But unlike in the human world where that would make the spouse a king and the children princes or princesses, we don't grant the husband any sort of royal status. He is given guardians to protect him, but is otherwise still just as he was before."

"So, Maivelynn is single by choice, not because she has to be?"

"Who said she was single?" Dez smiled as Allie stared. "Her husband prefers to stay out of the limelight and often travels to other parts of the realm to bring Queen Maivelynn news and various gifts. He loves to spoil her."

"Will I ever meet him?" Allie asked.

"Perhaps someday."

Chapter 26

After breaking down their campsite and returning everything as it had been, Allie and Dez prepared to continue their journey. Allie paused by Artemios and stroked his feathers. In the sunlight they were a soft gray with pearly white stripes. Only a hint of their glow lit her fingers as she touched him. "Pleasant dreams, Artemios," she said gently. "Thank you." She followed Dez through the woods. A dusting of snow and frost created a stunning picture on the leaves and bark of the trees they walked past. "Does it often snow this early in Summer Wood?" she asked.

"No, we usually don't get snow here until November," Dez replied. They'd reached the garage where his car waited with

Allie's Stingray next to it. He looked at her for a moment. "I don't suppose you'd like to drive today?"

"Really?" Allie asked. "You'd let me drive?"

He shrugged with a smile. "Sure. You know where you're going, right?"

"Yeah!" Her face fell. "But I don't have my keys."

Dez tossed them to her with a smile. "Your grandma gave these to me after she had the car brought here. I think she was afraid you might try to run away if she gave them to you."

"She might have been right," Allie admitted with a laugh. Suspicion clouded her face and she glared at Dez. "Who brought it?"

Shrugging again, he said, "Don't really know. I would guess your dad."

Too excited to stay suspicious long, Allie smiled and unlocked the doors to her car. She got in the driver's seat and with a contented sigh turned the ignition. "Ah, baby, I missed you."

Dez laughed. "I don't think I've ever heard a girl talk to her car like that before."

Smirking, Allie said, "I'm not like most girls."

"No, no you're not," he replied as they pulled out of the garage. "So, have you ever really opened her up, just to see what she could do? Or do you always follow the speed limit?"

"Just between us?" she asked.

"Just between us," he agreed.

She smiled as she turned onto the road into town. "Once a friend and I drove out to a fairly deserted old highway. Put the pedal to the metal and just let her run."

Dez chuckled. "So, how fast were you going?"

"Are you sure you want to know?" she asked with a wink.

"Oh, now I'm curious."

Allie laughed. "Got up to a hundred ten before my friend and I decided that maybe we were pushing our luck a little too far. Lucky for us that really is a deserted highway and there weren't any state troopers out."

"Like to live dangerously, huh?" Dez teased.

"Once in a while," Allie replied. "Life's too short to be serious all the time. But that story is absolutely not to go outside this vehicle."

"Wouldn't dream of it," he said with a grin. "I'm just enjoying the image of you speeding down the highway."

"Dad would probably kill me if he knew that story." She gave an impish grin. "He's always pushed following the laws and when I bought the car he told me that any shenanigans would end with him taking my keys and replacing my

Stingray with a junker. For the most part I keep myself out of trouble. But when you've got a ride like this one, at some point you have to find out what she can do."

Dez shook his head with a laugh. "Allie Jones, you are something else."

"And proud of it," she smirked. She glanced in the rearview mirror and noticed a glow around herself she'd never seen before. Realizing she was seeing her first glimpse of the Fey within her, Allie smiled. Soon they reached the apartment building and she turned to Dez. "Please lock your door. No automatic locks."

He nodded as he got out. "I think I'll let you go into your apartment to change and maybe grab an extra set of clothes or something. I'm going to stop by Cynthia Lampwick's and see if she's heard anything new since the last time we talked to her."

"You're just looking for cookies," Allie teased.

Dez shrugged. "Hey, a guy's gotta eat, right?"

"I guess so," she laughed.

As they walked toward her apartment, they saw Cynthia beckoning them from her door. When Dez started to open his mouth, she held a finger to her lips. "Come quickly," she whispered.

Dez and Allie looked at each other with frowns, but followed Cynthia's directions.

Once they were inside her apartment, she closed the door behind them and locked it. "Please, stay very quiet. Go wait in my room until they're gone."

"Who, Cynthia?" Dez asked.

"I don't know, but they're searching Allie's apartment right now. I think they know you brought her back here. Maybe they thought you left her here yesterday, fools. Please, into my room. Percy and I will ensure they do not come in here."

"I can help you," Dez began, but Cynthia stopped him.

"No, they must not know that either of you are here. I promise you, Percy and I can keep you safe. But you must wait where I asked you to." With surprising strength, she pushed Dez and Allie into her small bedroom. "Please, just stay here until I come get you," she whispered.

Allie's heart thundered in her ears. "Why are they so determined to take me?" she whimpered as she sank to the floor, wrapping her arms about herself.

"Shhh, Allie," Dez said, sitting next to her. "We'll figure this out. In the meantime, try to stay calm. Depending on who or what is out there, fear will only draw them closer."

"Right, because that makes me feel better," she muttered.

He put his arms around her shoulders and pulled her close, kissing her forehead. "Then let me help you," he whispered. He pushed the hair from her face and smiled. "We'll just pretend we're hanging out at the movies, or whatever people do for fun."

Allie couldn't help a small giggle. "Except there's no movie playing."

Dez shrugged. "Minor complication. So, what exactly do people do at the movies?"

"You've never been to the movies?" Allie asked quietly, pulling away to look at him.

"For the sake of conversation, let's say I haven't. What should we do?"

She frowned. "Didn't Cynthia tell us to be quiet?"

"We can whisper," Dez said with a mischievous grin. "Whispering is quiet."

Allie shook her head with a laugh. "Okay. Well, I guess the first question is are we at the movie with friends or is it just the two of us?"

"Does it make a difference?"

"Of course it does."

"Okay then, it's just the two of us," Dez replied. "What do

we do first?"

"We have to pick a movie. So are we watching a rom-com or an action flick?"

"You choose."

Allie giggled. "That's a dangerous option. A girl will almost always choose the rom-com."

"Action flick it is then," Dez teased with a wink.

"Since I tend to prefer those anyway, I'll go along with it," she retorted, grinning. "Now we stop by the concession stand and get popcorn to share and something to drink."

Dez reached into his bag. "Water and jerky close enough?"

Feigning annoyance, Allie whispered, "Oh, I suppose so."

He chuckled and handed her a flask before putting his arm back around her shoulders. "So, we've got snacks and we've picked a movie. Now what?"

Allie took a drink and leaned against Dez's shoulder. "We sit and wait for the movie to start."

"Just sit?" he asked. "That seems boring."

She turned to him, entranced by the honey-gold of his eyes. "Well, I suppose we don't have to just sit."

"No? What would you suggest we do instead?"

Allie couldn't think straight with him looking at her like that. She shrugged. "What do you want to do?"

He traced her jawline with a finger sending a thrill through her. "Now you're the one making a dangerous suggestion," he said quietly. "Anyone could tell you what a guy would say to that."

"What would he say?"

Rather than answer, Dez lowered his mouth to hers, kissing her gently. Warmth spread through Allie at the tender embrace. She had all but forgotten the danger they were in when a sudden crash outside the door forced them apart.

Chapter 27

Dez immediately pulled Allie toward Cynthia's small closet. "Stay here and don't move," he whispered urgently.

"But…"

"No, Allie, not this time," he replied. "Please, stay here. You can leave the door open unless you see me leave. Then shut it until I come back." He kissed her hand before leaving her in the closet and walking over to the bedroom door. He stood next to it with his hand poised above the doorknob, obviously listening. "That voice," he whispered. "It's familiar, but I can't tell."

At first, Allie couldn't hear anything. She thought about how focusing her sight allowed her to see others for what they were. She wondered if the same thing worked for her other senses. Allie closed her eyes, trying to bring her focus to what was going on outside the room. The words were faint at first, like the time she'd heard someone else's conversation on her phone while talking to a friend. But they gradually became clearer.

"I'm not sure why you believe such an important individual would come to see me," she heard Cynthia say.

A low voice, dripping with malice, sneered, "Do not lie to us, witch. We know she came yesterday."

"I'm a lonely old woman. The princess has been my neighbor for quite some time. So she visits me sometimes, I don't see how it's any business of yours."

"Where is she, Cynthia?"

To Allie's surprise, she heard Cynthia laugh. "How should I know where the princess spends her days? I'm certainly not privy to every detail of her life."

"She's here, isn't she?"

Allie covered her mouth to prevent crying out.

"Of course not," Cynthia replied with such conviction, Allie would have believed it herself if she wasn't huddled under the skirts hanging in Cynthia's closet. "I haven't seen her since her visit yesterday. It's a shame too. I've made some delightful molasses cookies. Perhaps you'd like to have some."

"I'm not interested in your cookies," the voice snapped. "If I were you, I would consider where my loyalties truly lie."

"My loyalties have been and will always be with the future of the Fey," Cynthia retorted. "The past holds nothing over me and the present is mine to live as I will."

"The past is our heritage, and you would do well to remember your own."

"Life is not lived in the past. We remember the past so we do not repeat the mistakes of yesterday, but we do not dwell there. We move forward, grow, and adapt. This is how the Fey have always lived."

"Not always," the voice sneered. "You of all people should know that. Tread carefully, Cynthia. We'll call again soon."

"I don't think you will. I have nothing of interest to you," she replied. Again, the persuasive tone of Cynthia's voice made Allie believe she truly didn't have any information. She didn't know anything of Allie or her whereabouts.

The voice laughed, a chilling sound that raised goosebumps over Allie's arms. "We'll see, witch."

Allie heard the door close and glanced at Dez. He shook his head. It wasn't long before Cynthia opened the door.

"Well, my dears, that was unpleasant. Come have some tea and cookies. I think we'd all feel better after a nice cup of chamomile." She led them back to the living room where Percy was lounging on the windowsill. "I'll just set up the teapot and we'll have ourselves another chat."

"Actually, are they gone enough that I can go to my apartment for a few moments? I haven't had a chance to get dressed for the day," Allie explained.

Cynthia looked her over. "I believe so, dear. Perhaps it would be best to send Dez over to pick some things up and you can stay here with me. You'd be welcome to shower and change in my bathroom."

The idea of Dez digging through her drawers to find a clothes didn't bother her until she remembered she would need fresh underwear as well. Dez certainly did not need to be looking through that drawer. Allie blushed. "I'd rather do it myself, Cynthia."

She smiled. "I understand. Yes, you should be safe going over. But be swift about it and take Percy along with you. He'll keep watch and ensure we don't have any repeat visitors."

The cat groaned. "But I just got comfortable."

"Then you can get comfortable again later," Cynthia

retorted without sympathy. "Right now, you are needed. If you wish to sit and complain, I can cancel my catnip order."

Percy slowly rose from his place and hopped to the floor. "All right, all right," he grumbled. "I'm going."

Dez stopped Allie at the door. "I can sit outside your apartment. You shouldn't go alone."

"I'm not going alone," she replied with a grin. "I've got Percy with me."

"You know…"

Allie held a finger to his mouth. "Yes, I know what you mean. I'll be fine. Just going to change into fresh clothes, grab a few essentials, and I'll be right back. You won't even miss me."

Dez snorted. "I doubt that, but fine. Just be careful, okay?"

"When am I not?" she retorted.

"Remember that story you told me on the way here?" he teased.

She smirked. "That story doesn't count because outside the car, it never happened."

He laughed and shook his head. "All right, you win. Just hurry."

Before she could talk herself out of it, Allie kissed his cheek and left Cynthia's apartment. She looked down the cement alleyway between the buildings. Not seeing anyone or anything, she walked to her own apartment where Percy sat, twitching his tail.

"You better be quick with those keys. The cement is cold and my whiskers are freezing."

"I didn't realize cats were so whiny," Allie muttered as she opened the door to her apartment.

Percy scoffed. "Cats are not whiny. We have high standards."

"That's just a fancy way of saying, 'We're whiny,'" Allie teased.

The cat yowled before slipping past her and running through the apartment. "Other than your dismal choice in decor, your apartment is safe. Do what you must so we can return to Cynthia's." He hopped onto the windowsill and proceeded to wash his paws.

Allie rolled her eyes before walking back to her bedroom. She stopped at the bathroom long enough for a fast shower. After blow-drying her hair, she brushed it and put it up into a ponytail. As she looked into the mirror, she remembered what Dez had told her. "Maybe if I just try harder." She focused in on her image. Slowly a faint glow grew around her and the top points of her ears elongated. The plain towel she'd wrapped around herself shimmered and changed to a flowing, long gown of teal blue. A sparkling gold circlet with tiny crystals appeared in her hair. "Wow," she whispered.

"Are you coming, princess?" Percy called from the hallway.

Remembering she still needed to change clothes, Allie looked away from the mirror. She changed quickly into jeans and a sweater before grabbing her jacket and boots out of the closet. Once dressed, she went back out to the living room.

Percy glared at her. "Took you long enough."

"Sorry, your highness," Allie retorted with a mock bow.

"Being snippy with me won't win you any favors."

Allie locked the door behind her before going back to Cynthia's apartment.

Dez was pacing the living room when she walked in. "What took you so long?"

"Are fairies and cats related? Because you have about the same patience," Allie scowled. "Believe it or not, it takes a little time to get ready for the day."

"Tea is ready," Cynthia said with a warm smile. "Let's sit down and relax together for a little bit."

Allie and Dez sat together on Cynthia's comfortable sofa while she took her seat in her weathered rocking chair. "We won't just be relaxing," Dez said. "We need to talk about who was at your door earlier."

Cynthia frowned. "Must you ruin the moment? We will discuss that, of course. But for now, let's just pretend that you are a sweet, young couple visiting an older woman in her loneliness."

The plate of cookies was nearly empty before Cynthia acknowledged that anything unpleasant had occurred. Dez attempted to bring it up several times and each time, Cynthia changed the subject so smoothly the topic was momentarily forgotten. While Dez picked up the last cookie on the plate, Allie had a sudden epiphany. "Cynthia, you're a descendent of Nyx, aren't you?"

Dez startled and nearly dropped his cookie. "That's ridiculous! She can't possibly be related to Nyx."

Cynthia smiled sadly. "Is it so hard to believe that someone good and kind could come from such a dark lineage, Dez? What our parents were, or our grandparents, or many great grandparents were isn't what we are destined to be, is it? If so, perhaps I have chosen the wrong side of this fight."

"How long have you known?" Allie asked as Dez opened and shut his mouth like a fish out of water.

"Oh, I've always known," Cynthia replied, setting down her teacup. "Where many of the Fey look constantly to the future, those of us from the Hollow have always done some searching of our past. It is how we learn the abilities of our magic and determine our paths. It was, perhaps, misleading of me to speak of Nyx and her daughters in the terms I did when we first met, but there is so much suspicion around her I felt it in my best interest to remain vague. Or rather to make it sound like information was unavailable. I am sorry. I've never had any desire to be like my ancestor. She allowed her power too great a hold on her and it destroyed her in the end. But she did have abilities I have benefited from by learning."

"You were able to convince your visitors that you knew nothing about my whereabouts. That's because of her persuasion."

"Not hers, mine," Cynthia corrected, "but the idea is the same. I've spent many years practicing the art of persuasion. And yes, it allowed me to keep your location a secret."

"But if you've been practicing persuasion, how do we know you haven't been tricking us?" Dez demanded.

With a shrug, Cynthia said, "I suppose you know because I say I haven't. It's up to you whether or not you believe me."

Dez opened his mouth, but Allie interrupted him, "If

you've known, why didn't you tell us?"

"Because of exactly what's happening right now. Before you knew, I was just a harmless old woman. Perhaps you even saw me a little like Glenda from *The Wizard of Oz*, a kindly witch who would help you find your way home. But now you see me in light of the past. Fear has entered you and you begin to question my motives and my actions."

"I'm not questioning you, Cynthia," Allie replied gently. "You've given me no reason not to trust you."

Cynthia smiled. "I appreciate the confidence, Allie." A frown tugged at her lips. "Unfortunately, Dez is correct. We must discuss what happened earlier. The person who came here was not from the Hollow. I have no doubt he was hired by someone there, but while I'm not entirely certain I got the sense I had known him before. The more I think of it, the more sure I am."

"Was he an elf? Blond hair, tall?" Dez asked.

Shaking her head, Cynthia said, "No. No, he was no elf." She looked out the window before turning back to Dez. "He was a fairy."

"A fairy?" Dez repeated.

"There could be no mistaking. But I fear he has turned to the imp's ways."

"A dark fairy then," Allie said.

"That is one way to think of it. Yes, that would be the perfect definition." Cynthia sighed and turned to Dez. "I'm very sorry, Dez, but I think you may have known who he was too. Deep green wings like yours, brown hair that is almost black, hazel eyes, and a scar across the left cheek."

Dez paled. "It can't be. He died years ago."

"No, Dez," Cynthia said quietly, "he didn't. Not if the one I saw today is in fact who I believe he was."

"Who?" Allie asked.

"Caspar Polanski," Cynthia replied.

In a voice barely audible, Dez said, "My brother."

Chapter 28

Shocked silence filled the room as Allie tried to wrap her mind around what had just been revealed. "Brother? You have a brother?"

"I once had three," Dez replied quietly. "I thought they'd all died in the..." His voice trailed away as he looked away from them.

"No, you're not getting away with going quiet on me now," Allie retorted, anger starting to build in her. "What happened? What was the experience that allowed you to be a guardian to the Princess of the Fey so young?"

Dez sighed. "The Fey Realm is beautiful, but it is also dangerous. When I was young, I lived in a part of the realm known as Wandwood Glade. It is where most of the fairies, pixies, and sprites make their homes. Or, it was."

"It is again, Dez," Cynthia said gently. "You just haven't returned since the dragon came."

"There's nothing there for me to go back to," he whispered.

"A dragon destroyed your home?" Allie guessed.

Dez shrugged, though it was a more defeated gesture than his normal, unbothered reaction. "If it was only that simple. One of the good things we talked about Nyx doing as queen was to create certain treaties with the dragons. Not all dragons are bad, some are very good, but it is generally understood that dragons are on the darker side of the Fey realm. They are powerful, and they know it. Being powerful can make one benevolent and wise, or it can lead to greed and malice. Maldran was in the latter category. For years, the dragons and the inhabitants of Wandwood Glade had an understanding. The dragons could come in the fall season to thin the deer herds and in exchange the fairies could gather mountainous herbs and berries from the regions they inhabited. They have similar understandings with other parts of the realm, so they always have a good hunting ground. Maldran decided it wasn't enough. He wanted the dragons to have access to

Wandwood Glade at any time."

"Can I ask the silly question of why they can't?"

"Same reason mortal hunters can't shoot deer year-round," he replied. "There is a time and season for it. Too early in the year leaves orphaned fawns who cannot survive without their mothers. And it wasn't just that he wanted constant access, he was also preparing to set restrictions on where and what we could gather in the mountains. Probably as the means to force his way, but my father wasn't going to be pushed around."

Allie frowned. "I'm confused. Why your father?"

"While Maivelynn is Queen of the Fey," Cynthia began, "each of the different parts of the realm has their own leader. The Hollow is led by Mathilda Powers. Wandwood Glade is led by a pixie named Serena Maizie."

"Couldn't Queen Maivelynn just stop them?" Allie asked. "She's the queen after all."

"The dragons have never fallen under the Queen of the Fey's rule," Dez replied. "They've always had their own laws, their own kings and queens. There are treaties between the two kingdoms to prevent the hostilities that used to plague the Fey Realm, but we have our conflicts just as in the mortal sphere. My father was the leader of Wandwood Glade. As with most small conflicts between peoples, he at first tried to reason with Maldran on his own. He didn't want to bother the queen if it was something he could resolve on his own. Several attempts to reach a compromise were made, but with no good solutions being found."

"Is that when Maldran attacked the forest?"

Dez shook his head with a bitter laugh. "Oh no. When Father saw he wasn't getting anywhere with Maldran, he sent a message to Queen Maivelynn requesting help. The queen agreed to come. They met together with King Maldran and we thought they'd been able to reach an agreement. We agreed to increase the hunt time to include part of the winter. And King Maldran agreed to uphold our original treaty allowing us to gather whatever herbs and berries we would find useful from the mountains."

For a long while, Dez sat silently, emotions chasing each other across his face and in his eyes. Allie put her hand on his knee. "He lied to you, didn't he?"

"Maldran knew Queen Maivelynn would stay in the glade overnight. Wandwood Glade is a ways from Summer Wood. I suppose he thought by removing both the Queen of the Fey and Wandwood Glade's leader, he could get away with taking over our part of the realm. It's no secret the dragons want the woods for themselves, if for nothing else than the food supply.

I don't know, maybe he wanted the whole Fey Realm to himself."

"How many dragons followed him?"

"The strange thing?" Dez replied. "None. I don't think he realized how out of touch with his own kind he had become. While the dragons want to have the forest, most of them follow the treaties as outlined because they see how it benefits everyone. They are, for the most part, an honorable race. No, Maldran came alone. But even just one dragon can wreak untold damage. He came at midnight."

Dez fell silent again, tears shimmering in his eyes. Cynthia leaned forward in her rocker to pat his knee. "I'll continue the story, Dez." She looked at Allie. "I'm sure you've seen forest fires before?"

Allie nodded. She didn't trust her voice.

"Dragon fire has been responsible for many of them. Not all, mind you. There are still cases of careless humans destroying nature's beauty. And of course there is the occasional lightning strike. But many fires which have been attributed to natural causes were the work of dragons. I don't think they always mean to do it. After all, a dragon can't help their heat and fire. But in this case, the fire was intentional. Maldran started at the far edges of the glade before turning to the center."

"He tried to block any escape," Allie said, eyes wide.

Cynthia gave a sad nod. "The fairies and sprites nearest the edges immediately set to putting the fires out, but they had no way of knowing Maldran was heading further inside and so no message was sent to Marco Polanski or the queen." She paused and shook her head. "It was a terrible thing. So many innocent lives lost. Centuries' worth of precious trees destroyed. History and memories forgotten. As soon as Marco heard the dragon's roar, he set out to protect first the queen and then his people. It's a tough call when one has no warning a disaster is coming. The queen wanted to stay and help Marco, but he insisted she flee. Dez was sent with the queen for his safety. Then Marco and his three oldest sons joined the fight against the dragon."

"Not that it helped," Dez retorted.

"You're still here, aren't you?" Cynthia pointed out, a chiding tone to her voice. "But it is true. The fight was vain. Maldran was too powerful for the little band of warriors. How Caspar survived is a tale he'd have to tell himself, because I truly don't know. In fact, he's been believed to be dead since the battle. When the dragon had finished with the warriors, he pursued Queen Maivelynn. A unicorn is fast, but not fast enough to outrun a malevolent dragon. When Maldran caught up to them, Lord Nightwind fought as best he could. It was clear the unicorn was no match for the dragon. But something unexpected happened. A thirteen-year-old fairy joined the fight."

Allie glanced over at Dez, who was sitting with his face to the floor. He had only been thirteen? At thirteen she was dreaming of fairy tales and struggling to figure out where she fit in her middle school's pecking order. She didn't have to worry about her home being invaded, or worse destroyed.

"His only weapon was a small bow with arrows. Hardly the best weapon of choice when fighting a dragon. But his aim was unsurpassed. He found the weak spot in the dragon's armor and took the shot. Maldran was defeated, but at a terrible cost. Much of the glade burned long into the night and the remaining inhabitants were forced to flee. Queen Maivelynn took the young fairy with her when they discovered his family had perished. And with Lord Nightwind's recommendation, Dezydery Polanski began training to be a Guardian of the Realm."

They sat in silence for a long while, Allie trying to absorb everything she'd just learned. Perhaps this was part of why her parents had kept her from the Fey Realm for so long. Who would want their child growing up in fear of such terror?

"If Caspar truly is alive, I have to find him," Dez said finally. "I have to find out why he never came to find me. And why for the love of all that is good he would ally himself with darkness. That doesn't sound like the brother I knew."

"Tragedy changes people in many different ways, Dez," Cynthia replied gently. "For some, it makes them stronger. But others become bitter. And bitterness will never lead a person to the light."

Chapter 29

Allie and Dez knew they couldn't stay at Cynthia's apartment long. They finished their snack before getting up to leave. "Are you sure you'll be okay here?" Dez asked. "We can send a guardian to stay with you until this mess gets straightened out."

"Actually, I've been thinking of visiting Hazel for a while," Cynthia replied. "No better time than the present, is there? Perhaps, since I'm sure you'll be returning to Summer Wood, I can accompany you as far as the forest. We can then separate once we reach the woods. Percy and I know our way to the palace and I'm sure you two would like to continue your investigation without an old woman slowing you down."

Something in the way Cynthia said those words made Allie pause. Before she knew what was coming out of her mouth, she blurted, "You should join us."

Dez and Cynthia both stared at her. "What?" they said in unison.

Allie stammered for a moment, "Well, it's just that, you know, we've heard witches have excellent hearing, which would be really useful. And you obviously care deeply about us since you worked so hard to keep us safe. And there's your cookies. I don't think Dez could survive without your cookies." She glanced desperately at Dez who was looking at her like she had two heads. She resisted the urge to stamp her foot in frustration. Instead she sighed and said, "You're not that old, Cynthia, and you'd be a help. I'm sure of it."

Cynthia laughed. "My dear girl, you needn't worry about me feeling useful. I have some ideas which, with Hazel's help, could lead to some sort of breakthrough on how we can prevent this kerfluffle from becoming a tragedy."

"Kerfluffle?" Dez repeated.

"Yes. Other than your unfortunate injuries, thinking of which, dear, you really should be putting some kind of salve on those wings if you want them to heal faster, both of you have come through this far without lasting harm. Attempts to thwart you have been soundly defeated. Why, compared to most similar situations, this has been a walk in the park. Anyhow, I will visit Hazel. Perhaps, we can arrange a meeting to exchange ideas and information? I'm sure Hazel has access to a kitchen and I can make fresh cookies for you," Cynthia added with a wink.

"That does make more sense," Dez said, looking at Allie.

Allie looked between the two of them. The now familiar tingling sensation of her own Fey power grew. "Cynthia, I really feel like you should join us. At least for today. I don't know why we need you, to be completely honest. And I know you still feel like you would somehow hamper us. But you're wrong. We need you and we need your help. Please."

Cynthia bowed slightly. "Very well, my princess, I shall join you today. Understand though, my dear, I do have plans of my own regarding this mess and I need to be able to consult with my cousin on how best to proceed."

"That's fine," Allie said. "Thank you."

Smiling, Cynthia said, "Hear that, Percy? You're in for a rough day."

The cat stretched on the windowsill and turned slightly. "And who said I would be coming?"

"I did, you nincompoop," Cynthia retorted.

Percy flicked his tail and yawned. "Um, no thanks. Someone should stay here and protect the apartment."

"Not an option, Percy. Now come help me get some things packed for our journey."

As Cynthia and Percy went into her room, Percy grumbling the entire way, Dez moved closer to Allie. His voice came in a low whisper as he asked, "What was that all about?"

Allie sighed. "I don't know, Dez, but we need her with us. I do know that much."

"We would travel faster on our own," he pointed out. "Cynthia is spry and all, but she's also being honest. She's getting old and won't be able to travel as quickly as you or I."

"Perhaps," she admitted, "but I'm not willing to take that chance. Something tells me we'll need her. I can't explain it and I'm not going to try. Just trust me on this."

Dez shook his head. "How can I not when you've got your whole Princess of the Fey thing going?"

"You can see a difference?"

"See it, hear it, everything about you changes when you take that role and use it," Dez replied. "It's a rather remarkable thing to see."

She blushed and looked away from him. Then turned back. "Do you go through a similar change? When you use your role as guardian?"

Dez shrugged. "I really wouldn't know. The times I've been acting in my role I haven't been in a position to see myself. I would imagine everyone does though. It's probably subtle for most Fey, but the very fact that you are destined to be queen someday makes yours a little more spectacular. Even Queen Maivelynn changes when she fully takes on her role."

"I don't think I've ever seen her do that."

"It's not really something you want to see. Typically when the Queen of the Fey uses her power, the situation is pretty dire."

"Have you ever seen her do that?"

"Once," Dez replied, his eyes far away. "The night Maldran was defeated."

~*~

It was easy to forget they were on a dangerous mission with Cynthia and Percy in the backseat of the Stingray. Cynthia had been giddy as a schoolgirl when they'd walked to the car. "Oh, I haven't seen one of these in ages!" she squealed. "And I've never gotten to ride in one."

"How have you not seen it since I moved in?" Allie asked.

"I never go out by the parking lot," Cynthia admitted. "I choose other methods of travel when I must be out and about." She continued to chat easily as they drove back toward the forest. Percy muttered about everything they passed and eventually stopped talking all together to take a nap in Cynthia's lap.

Allie was about to turn into the forest when Dez said, "Keep going straight."

"But we need to go inside, don't we?"

"Yes, but we're going to take a back way. Just keep going straight for a while. I'll tell you when to turn."

Trusting her guardian, Allie continued down the road. The trees grew more gnarled as they moved along. Darkness fell over them. The few leaves clinging to their branches shuddered in the light breeze.

"Are you sure you want to go this way, dear?" Cynthia asked. "There is a reason this entrance is not used often."

Dez nodded. "I'm sure. It's obvious that whoever was behind Allie's attempted kidnapping was not fooled by us leaving in the night. Otherwise there would have been no visitors to your door, Cynthia. They'll be watching the typical paths into the forest. This one is dangerous, but less likely to be watched for just that reason."

"I hope you know what you're doing," Allie muttered.

"So do I."

Chapter 30

Dez pointed out a small shed where Allie could park the Stingray. Cynthia clutched her small bag close as they got out of the car and looked at the forest. If the regular entrance was eerie, this point was forbidding. The light breeze which surrounded them with the scent of earth and trees died at the tree line, leaving it strangely motionless. No bird calls filled the air. Allie saw no deer, squirrels, or even insects lingering nearby. It was as though the area was completely abandoned except for the silent trees keeping guard. "Be as quiet as possible," Dez whispered. "With any luck, our presence will go unnoticed."

"I learned long ago not to trust to luck, fairy," Percy

retorted, hopping from the car and strolling into the forest. "Well, what are you waiting for?" he called.

Cynthia rolled her eyes. "Stupid cat," she muttered before following him into the trees.

Dez took Allie's hand. "Whatever happens, follow my directions exactly, okay?"

She nodded. "I think I can do that."

"I mean it, Allie," he said urgently. "If I tell you to run, you run. Without worrying about me or what might be happening behind you."

She gave him a light kiss. "If you say run, I'll run. But I won't promise not to worry. I care about you."

He leaned his forehead against hers. "I care about you too. That's why I'm telling you to keep yourself safe, no matter what."

Without waiting for her to reply, Dez pulled her hand gently and they stepped into the forest. Silence clung to the air, making every crunch of a twig sound loud in Allie's ears. The stillness threatened to take the very breath from her as they moved forward. A strange swooping sound caused Dez to push Allie behind himself while Cynthia opened her bag.

"My princess! I am so very pleased to have found you at last," a familiar voice called.

"Artemios?"

The hercinia landed on a branch nearby. "Naturally. You have no idea how I worried when you were gone from camp this morning without so much as a fare thee well." He gave her a look mixed with reproach and affection. Then he looked at the forest around them. "Though I must say, you have chosen a rather dreary path through the forest this morning."

"We don't have much option, Artemios," Allie replied.

"No, indeed you do not. There are foul creatures in the Summer Wood. I came to give you warning against them."

"What are they?" Dez asked.

Artemios turned to him. "Creatures of darkness unlike anything I have before set my eyes on. They hide in the shadow and move like hares, but have horns like deer."

Allie giggled. "Jackalopes?"

"Do not underestimate them, my princess," Artemios chided.

"Rabbits with horns aren't going to be all that dangerous, Artemios," Allie replied with a laugh. "I didn't realize they were real too, but I suppose it makes sense with everything else I've learned. Jackalopes are the staple of American legends. I've never heard of them being anything but cute and fluffy. Hardly a threat."

Dez suppressed a laugh of his own. "Well, it does depend on the legend. Some say they will attack and gore hunters, but since we're not hunting them, I can't see them hurting us."

Artemios cocked his head. "You truly do not believe we should be concerned about these creatures?"

"I wouldn't say that," Cynthia replied, coming over with Percy. "Jackalopes prefer to go unseen and aren't often found in Summer Wood. They prefer the more desert regions. I have to wonder why there are suddenly jackalopes outside their normal habitat."

"You do have a point," Dez admitted. "I guess the best thing to do would be to try talking to one of them."

"That shouldn't be too hard," Percy drawled. "There's one hiding in the bush over there."

"Mangy cat!" a voice yelled. "Why'd ya go and turn me in?"

"We only want to talk to you. Will you come out?" Dez asked.

"Not with that hawk sittin' there," the voice replied. "Tell it to go away and I might."

Artemios glowered, but Allie said, "Why don't you fly somewhere nearby so you can catch up with us more easily?"

"Very well, Your Highness."

He flew away and a jackalope hopped out from behind the bush, pounding her foot on the ground.

Allie stared. The jackalope's tan and white fur was mottled and dusty. She stood about the height of a German shepherd with antlers similar to a pronghorn's growing from her head. Dark eyes glowered at them. She was easily twice the size of the fake taxidermy jackalopes Allie had seen in tourist shops.

"Um, we're not going to hurt you," Allie said finally.

"Hmph, that's what everybody says," the jackalope retorted bitterly. "Then they go 'n' haul off yer whole fam'ly."

Allie and Dez glanced at each other. Dez cleared his throat. "I'm Dez and this is Allie. We're really not interested in hurting you, Miss…"

"Missus, thank you very much. Mrs. Tallulah Hare." She glared at them. "May as well call me Tallulah. Whaddya want?"

"We're just curious what you're doing here near Summer Wood, Tallulah," Dez replied. "Don't you normally prefer being farther south?"

"Well it certainly weren't my idea to move up here," she snapped. "Too dang cold. But the mister says we had to go. Too many people around. And them dogs was gettin' unbearable."

"Dogs?" Allie asked.

"Vicious vermin," Tallulah spat. "Always comin' out at night. Fangs drippin' foam and all, from what I hear'd. You'd think they was rabid. They tear up a burrow faster'n you could blink. All that'd be left is mangled twigs and bloody bits of fur. My Henry says it was time to go somewhere safer, so he picked this awful place. S'pose it's better'n havin' them dogs after us."

Dez frowned. "Tallulah, can you tell us more about these dogs. What did they look like?"

"I ain't never got near enough to know. If you can find her, Susie Marsh lost her brood to them dogs. Maybe she can help you. Henry says we's gonna find the Queen of the Fey here and see if she can't help us. Seems downright cowardly to run away, but I gotta think about my babies, don't I?"

"How many of you are going to see the queen?" Allie asked.

"Oh ever'body who got out is comin'. I reckon there's a good three dozen families travelin' this way."

Dez's eyes widened, but he said, "Well, if you see Susie, would you ask her to come talk to us? I'd like to know more about these dogs."

"You ain't got dogs like that here, do ya?" Tallulah asked suspiciously.

"Not that I've ever seen," Dez replied. "But I'd be able to tell you more if I knew what type of dogs you were dealing with."

Tallulah nodded. "I'll tell her if I see her. Take care, y'all." She then turned and hopped away with more speed than Allie would have guessed from an animal that size. As soon as she was gone, Artemios flew back to his branch.

"This is not good," Dez murmured. "Three dozen families of jackalopes coming? And at this time of year?"

"What's the problem?" Allie asked. "They're just looking for somewhere safe to live."

"The problem is jackalopes breed just like any other rabbit out there," Dez retorted. "Three dozen families will decimate the food supply, especially as colder weather sets in. She thinks it's bad now, but you and I both know what will happen as the year wanes. They're going to starve."

"Interesting that they're coming to see the queen about dogs," Cynthia mused. "Regular dogs would probably never go near a jackalope burrow. The prey is too big for the trouble you'd have catching it."

Dez nodded. "That's why I was hoping she could give us

more information. I have a hunch someone sent black hounds to Fey Desert."

Artemios squawked. "Why would someone do that?"

"To cause a panic, though I'm not sure what the purpose would be," Dez replied.

Cynthia frowned. "Have there been other incidences recently of creatures less able to fend for themselves coming to Summer Wood?"

Dez thought for a moment. "Come to think of it, there have been several of the smaller Fey coming. Though certainly not in the same quantity we're seeing the jackalopes come. Why? What are you thinking?"

"They're setting the stage," Allie said quietly. "My attempted kidnapping, driving the small Fey from their normal habitat, framing the Council members. Whoever is behind this doesn't just want a quiet takeover. They're going to go in with a bang and they want everyone to see it."

Chapter 31

Silence fell as Allie's revelation hovered between them. "That is logical," Artemios said. "However, if that is the case, we must continue to the palace forthwith. The queen will have need of us."

Dez shook his head. "Yesterday Queen Maivelynn told us she wanted to proceed as though we hadn't learned of any sort of plot. She told us to focus on finding the would-be kidnapper as that would lead us to the actual person behind all this. As much as I hate to admit it, her plan does give us a slight edge."

"I don't think so, Dez," Allie replied. "The queen is operating in much the same way we did last night. Because we know someone was looking for me this morning, we know no one was fooled by my disappearance overnight. At least, not the right people. I think Artemios is right. We need to get back to Summer Wood and find out what we can do to help."

"Finding the elf who tried to kidnap you would help her," Dez pointed out. "Finding Caspar would help too. I can't believe he would turn to an imp. But if he has, I need to find out why. I need to know who turned him against his own people."

Allie sighed. "Dez…"

A strange grunt sounded nearby and Percy arched his spine with a hiss. "We've lingered too long."

Crashing footsteps came nearer while trees cracked. "What is that?" Allie asked.

Cynthia gasped. "Run, my children. Run!"

Dez changed to his fairy form, his sword appearing in his hand. "I'm not leaving you to battle a troll alone."

"You don't have a choice, Dez," Cynthia snapped. "You are in no condition to fight."

"I'm always in condition for a fight," Dez retorted, though Allie could see a flicker in his form. His wings showed tears which were only partially healed.

"Let's go, Dez," Allie said. "Cynthia can handle this."

"Are you crazy?" Dez asked.

She looked him straight in the eye as the sensation of her power grew. "We're going to leave this in Cynthia's hands with our blessing. She will more than manage."

"You won't be going anywhere if you two don't leave soon," Percy growled. Allie startled. The cat had grown into a sleek, powerful panther. He bared his fangs. "Run!"

The troll knocked over trees near them and Allie saw it fix its eyes on them. It roared, the thunderous noise echoing painfully in Allie's ears. She grabbed Dez's hand to begin pulling him away. "We need to go."

He yanked back from her. "Only a coward flees. I am a Guardian of the Fey and I will not turn my back on those who need me."

Cynthia's voice filled the forest as she opened her bag and pulled from it a long, wooden staff. "One chance, troll, go back to your cave."

The troll lifted a tree trunk overhead and swung it like a club. Dez pushed Allie to the ground to prevent her being knocked over with it. "You promised to follow my directions, Allie, and I'm telling you now to run as soon as the opportunity presents itself. Leave me with Cynthia. The two of us can outmatch a troll, but by herself I don't think she can."

"I never used the word 'promise,' Dez," Allie replied. "And I won't leave without you. Cynthia told us both to run. You're just being stubborn."

"Look who's talking," he muttered. "I can't leave her to defend us alone."

"She isn't alone." Allie heard a panther scream and watched Percy launch himself at the troll. The beast roared as Percy clawed his way up the troll's back and leaped off. Blasts of light hit the troll as Cynthia threw spells at it. "There isn't time to argue, Dez. Either we both go, or we both stay."

He cursed under his breath. "Fine, but so help me Allie if you get hurt or killed…"

Allie didn't give him a chance to finish his threat. She pulled his face to hers and kissed him soundly. "Now, let's go defeat a troll." She jumped to her feet. "I'll distract it. You and Cynthia do your stuff."

"You're going to do what now?"

Not bothering to repeat herself, Allie ran at the troll. She didn't know how to fight and she didn't have any spells to use, but she did know how to irritate people and was a fast runner. Grabbing a stone from the forest floor, she threw it as hard as she could at the troll's head. It bounced harmlessly off, but did get its attention. "Too slow to catch me!" she yelled. As soon as the troll moved her direction, she started sprinting away from it.

Percy took advantage of the distraction to pounce on the troll's back. He sank his teeth into its shoulder.

The troll roared and grabbed Percy with its other hand. With a growl, it threw Percy into the nearby trees with a sickening crunch. It then turned on Allie as Dez ran in with his sword.

Cynthia's staff glowed with brilliant light. She began chanting and the light gathered at the end of the staff, crackling with power. "And now, we finish this," she said in a deadly whisper that somehow carried over the din. A ball of light and energy shot from the staff, hitting the troll in the chest. It roared as stone encased its shrinking body. In moments it was only the size of a small pebble. Dez and Allie stared at it before turning to Cynthia who swayed slightly. Dez hurried to catch her arm. "I'm so sorry, my dears. I haven't done a spell that powerful in years. It is somewhat draining." She put the staff back into the bag, though Allie couldn't imagine how it had fit in there in the first place. "Where's Percy?"

"Here, my lady," Artemios called sadly from his perch in

the tree. Unequipped for a battle, he had occasionally swooped through but mostly stayed out of the way to allow the others to fight unhampered.

Cynthia moved with surprising speed to the place Percy lay. Tears filled her eyes as she examined his broken body. "Oh, Percy."

Allie knelt next to the big cat. "Maybe I can help him," she whispered. But as she looked, she knew what little experience in veterinary medicine she had wouldn't be enough. The injuries Percy had sustained were far beyond her abilities. She doubted she would have been able to help him even if she were fully trained. Not without tools and an animal hospital. When Cynthia looked at her hopefully, Allie dropped her eyes to the ground and shook her head.

"Got my wish," Percy rasped.

"What wish, dear?" Cynthia asked, stroking his magnificent head.

"Today I repaid my debt to you," Percy said, his mouth twitching in a slight smile. "And I got to do it in my true form. It would have been embarrassing to attempt to defeat a troll as merely a cat."

Cynthia choked in what was half sob and half laugh. "I've always seen you as your true self. You've never been merely a cat to me."

Percy grimaced. "No, I suppose not. I will miss your molasses cookies."

"No, Percy. What am I supposed to do without you?" she cried.

His lips twitched again. "Steal another neglected wild cat, of course."

"I didn't steal you, I rescued you," Cynthia corrected, though with a wry smile.

"Perhaps a tiger this time. You know the one I'm speaking of."

"Yes," Cynthia whispered as she nodded.

Percy turned his pale gaze to Allie. "Take care of my lady for me. I'm sorry I couldn't do more, princess."

Allie sniffled back tears of her own. "You did more than could ever have been asked. Thank you."

With one last glance at his mistress, Percy whispered, "I'll be waiting for you." His last breath sighed from him as Cynthia sobbed and wrapped her arms around him.

Chapter 32

After taking the time to bury Percy in the woods, Allie and the others continued their journey. Allie put a comforting arm around Cynthia's shoulders. "I'm so sorry, Cynthia."

The older woman sniffled. "I should have known better than to give a troll any opportunity. They are stupid creatures incapable of thought, even for their own self-interest."

"But Percy died the hero he'd always wanted to be," Allie said. "What did he mean by his debt was repaid?"

Cynthia sighed. "I rescued him from one of those so-called sanctuaries. Before you think I disapprove of all of them, that's not the case. So many people are trying to help our wild friends and I think that's a wonderful thing. Unfortunately, there are also many cases of people creating their own menageries under the guise of calling it a rescue. I found Percy locked in a cage far too small for him, his ribs showing because he hadn't been fed enough. It was plain he wasn't being treated well and he was sick. I promised him a comfortable home with me, in exchange for the slight indignity of spending most of his time as a regular house cat. After all, I probably wouldn't be able to convince the apartment management to allow me to keep a panther in the building, no matter how persuasive I was. He told me anything would be better than living in squalor. So I made the transformation and he easily fit through the bars. It took several weeks to nurse him back to full health. Anytime I came to the Hollow, Percy would accompany me and I'd allow him time as himself. Though as much as he complained about it, I think he rather enjoyed being a pampered pet at my apartment." She sighed again. "He made a great house cat. Never had a problem with mice, or really any sort of unwanted guests, and never lacked for company. I shall miss him greatly."

Allie patted Cynthia's arm. "I am sorry."

"Thank you, dear."

They walked in silence for a while before Allie said, "I just have to know. How do you manage to keep that staff in such a tiny bag?"

Cynthia laughed. "I am a witch, dear. Making sure I have everything I need in a convenient and lightweight bag is essential. You probably wouldn't believe how much stuff I have in this little purse." After a moment, she turned to Allie. "So, what do you plan to do about all of this?"

"We're going to find out who is causing these problems and we're going to stop them."

"Easier said than done."

Allie nodded. "But we have no other choice. We can't just sit by and let this happen." She paused when Dez stopped in front of them, holding a hand up. "What's the matter?"

"Do you smell that?" he asked quietly.

The two women sniffed. "It smells like smoke," Allie said.

"But there's no fire," Cynthia added. "Someone has had a campfire recently."

Dez nodded. "That's what I was thinking. If we're quiet and swift, we might be able to find the person who built it."

"I shall fly ahead and see what I can see," Artemios offered.

"Great, we'll follow," Allie replied.

The hercinia flew ahead of them, occasionally dropping

feathers when he changed directions. Dez made sure they left enough space between themselves and Artemios to allow him to properly scout the forest. After a moment, Dez motioned for them to stop. "We'll wait here until Artemios returns. If he does find someone, we don't want to barge in suddenly. We need to go in with a plan."

The minutes crawled until Artemios flew back to them, landing on a branch nearby. "I believe I have found our quarry."

"Our what?" Allie asked.

"Those whom we seek. They are in a clearing about sixty yards hence."

"They?" Dez repeated. "How many are there?"

"Three. A dark elf and an imp, both male, and there is a woman with them. She must be a witch as I sense great power about her. I would say the woman is their leader, based on what little I could hear of their discussion. She was speaking about a plan being placed in motion soon, but I'm afraid I could not get too much from the conversation. I did not wish to draw attention to myself and the darkness made it impossible for me to get close enough to hear everything," Artemios explained.

"That's all right, Artemios," Dez said. "Even just that will help us know how best to proceed. If the woman is in fact their leader, it would be best if we approach quietly and wait for her to leave before making any attempt to confront the others."

"The fact that she could well be a witch throws in another complication," Cynthia pointed out. "Witches have exceptional hearing. A bird flying past isn't going to draw attention, but the sound of three people walking towards her? I think it would be best if I went forward. I'm light on my feet for an old woman, and being a witch I wouldn't have to get as close in order to hear what was being discussed. As soon as I think she's preparing to leave, I can return to you and then we can attempt a confrontation, if that's truly what you think is wisest."

"She's got a good point," Allie said.

Dez eyed Cynthia warily. "You've misled us once."

"A mistake I will not repeat," Cynthia replied. "I believe I've more than proved myself worthy of your trust, Dezydery Polanski."

"Let her go, Dez," Allie pleaded. "Neither of us could hope to get the information she'll be able to without running the risk of getting caught."

Without speaking, Dez nodded and Cynthia smiled. She

muttered a few words and became a butterfly before flitting away.

Dez and Allie sat quietly while Artemios rested on his branch. The sun dipped slightly to the west and Allie's stomach growled, reminding her that she hadn't yet eaten lunch. Dez tossed her a piece of jerky. "I'm afraid I don't have much more than that, but at least it should make the grumblies go away."

Allie giggled. "The grumblies?"

Blushing, Dez shrugged. "That's what my dad called them when I was little."

"I think it's cute," Allie said.

While they sat quietly, Allie looked around. The forest in this area was quiet, but not eerily so. Birds fluttered in the treetops and through the woods. Rabbits and squirrels bounded along the forest floor. Everything seemed so normal. She had to admit, part of her missed being just normal. Not having to worry about magical beings chasing after her or threatening to destroy a world she hadn't known about. "Do you ever wonder how your life would have been different if you were just normal?"

Dez shrugged. "Not really. To me, this is normal."

"But do you ever stop and think about what would be

different if you were just a plain, ordinary mortal? No magic, no monsters?"

"Even the mortal world has monsters, Allie," Dez replied. "You just call them by different names."

She sighed. "I guess."

"I'm happy the way I am," Dez said at length. "And as difficult as life in the Fey Realm can be, I wouldn't trade it for any amount of plain ordinary. Because the truth is, no one is plain and ordinary. Not even mortals. And especially not princesses who thought they were ordinary."

Allie smiled, but didn't have a chance to respond as Cynthia suddenly reappeared before her, clutching her chest. "Cynthia, are you okay?"

"Just in shock, dear, but otherwise fine. I would never have believed it of her."

"Believed it of whom?" Artemios asked.

Cynthia looked at Allie, her eyes wide. "The witch leading them. I can't understand it. After all Hazel has done for her to be so ungrateful. After everything the queen has done for us!"

"Who?" Dez demanded.

"Lady Xylia."

"Lady Xylia? As in from the Fey Council?" Allie asked.

"There could be no mistaking her," Cynthia replied sadly.

"I could hardly believe my eyes when I saw her there."

"Their plan," Dez said, "did you hear anything about their plan?"

Cynthia shook her head. "I think they were wrapping up as I arrived. Xylia didn't stay long. All I know is they're going to do something tonight. Allie, I know you wanted me to stay with you through the day, but I must go to Hazel. If anyone can help us stop Xylia, it would be my cousin."

Allie nodded. "Yes, you must go to her. And we must go to the queen. She has to be warned."

"There's only one problem," Dez said. "We have no proof. I mean, yes, we've got eye-witness accounts, but for something of this magnitude, we're going to need more than that. We need actual proof that Lady Xylia has been behind this plot. Otherwise, the Fey Council will never take our word over hers. Especially if she practices persuasion. I assume she is also one of Nyx's descendants?"

Cynthia gave a small shrug. "I truly do not know since I've not taken the time to research both daughters' lines. I have only done work with Patience as she is my direct ancestor. And even then, it is hard to pinpoint exactly where everyone fits in the family tree. But I think it would be safe to work under the assumption that she is somehow related. It would match with the gossip going around the Hollow."

"So what do we do now?" Allie asked.

"If I may be so bold as to offer a suggestion," Artemios said, "you've pointed out that proof is required. If you were to capture even just one of her henchmen, that might help provide more information which you could use to your benefit."

Dez nodded. "That would be the best thing to do. If Lady Xylia has already gone, I doubt the elf and imp would have stayed long after. We should try to get at least one of them. Both would be better."

"Or you could wait for us to catch you."

Chapter 33

Allie spun around with the others to face the two men facing them. One was the dark elf who had attempted to kidnap her in Silver Quill Gifts. The other she hadn't met before, but she guessed by Dez's sharp intake of breath who it was.

"Caspar," Dez said through grit teeth.

For a moment, the imp appeared startled. But he quickly smoothed over it with a dark grin. "Miss me, little brother?"

"Certainly more than you missed me," Dez replied, bitterness sharpening his tone.

Caspar frowned, but didn't say anything as the dark elf sneered, "Well, since we're all together now, we'll be taking the princess with us. She has a very important audience with the queen, after all."

"You won't be taking her anywhere," Dez retorted.

The elf laughed. "Do you really think you can stop us? You got lucky earlier, fairy, because I wasn't supposed to take her then. But now, there is no stopping me. I have orders to take Allisatravondaresta Jones to the palace for a very special ceremony."

Shudders ran down Allie's spine at the tone in the elf's voice. "I don't go anywhere with people I don't know," she said, hoping her voice wasn't quivering as much as her knees were. "If you want me to go anywhere with you, you're going to have to introduce yourself."

He laughed again. "With or without it, you will come with me. But I suppose proper introductions are in order." He mocked a bow. "I'm called Eldred. But I already know who you are, so we can end the formalities there." Darkness gathered around him. "Now, you can come with me quietly and your friends will be spared. Or, you can attempt a fight in which case, they'll all die. What's it going to be, princess?"

Allie wasn't foolish enough to believe he'd actually let Dez and Cynthia go. But she wondered if she could buy them a little time by acting the willing victim. Before she could make any sort of reply, Artemios gave a shrill call and swooped at Eldred's face. The elf threw his arms up to protect himself as Artemios cried, "Flee, Your Highness!"

"But..."

"No buts this time, child," Cynthia said as she pulled her staff from her purse. "Run!"

Not waiting to be told again, Allie took off through the woods. Artemios soon appeared just ahead of her. "Follow me, Allie, and I shall lead you to a safe haven."

"Is there such a place anymore?" she asked.

"There is always a haven if one knows where to look for it," Artemios replied. "Now let us be swift!"

Allie tried to ignore the sounds behind her as she followed the hercinia deeper into the forest. Branches pulled at her clothes and scratched her skin as she sprinted past them. *If there is any power in me at all*, she thought, *please keep my friends from harm.* She hardly recognized the tingling within her as her legs ached. She hadn't run this much in a long time, and certainly not while dodging trees and bushes.

Artemios came to a stop before a thick oak tree. He pecked at a small knot high in the tree and a small opening appeared. "You must stay here, Allie. Dez will know where to find you."

"You're not going to leave me alone, are you?" Allie squeaked.

"I must, my princess," he said, his voice grave "Your friends have need of me. Stay here. This will be a safe haven so long as you remain inside. If you come out, you will not be able to reach the secret knot to let yourself back in." He brushed her cheek with his wing. "Take three of my tail feathers. They shall give you a little light as you wait."

As gently as she could, Allie pulled three feathers from Artemios' tail. "Are you sure about this? Isn't there something I can do to help?"

"Remaining safe is the best help you can be, Allie," he said. "Now I must go. Stay within the haven and do not come out for anything. Dez or I will open the tree to release you when the time is right."

Allie nodded and placed her back against the soft wood. Slowly the tree closed around her. The tail feathers in her hand glowed and she discovered there was air moving through the inside of the tree from an opening near the top of the trunk. She could hear the wind rustling the leaves above her. Occasionally sunlight broke through the clouds enough to give the small space extra light. Allie tried to ignore the rapid beating of her heart. She'd never liked being in enclosed spaces and the tree trunk wasn't nearly large enough for her taste. She focused her hearing outside the tree and closed her eyes, hoping she could imagine herself out in the woods. Birdsong played sweetly in her ears. She heard squirrels and chipmunks scamper up the trunk of the tree. The woodsy scent of the oak filled her nostrils with each breath she took. Slowly her heart rate slowed to normal and she began to relax. Allie hoped her friends were all right as she continued to wait for someone to show up. Part of her hated sitting in the tree while the others were fighting for her safety. But Artemios was right. If she could stay out of enemy hands, they would have a greater chance of succeeding against Lady Xylia and those plotting with her.

She still couldn't believe the council member was the one behind the plot. From everything Allie had seen, Queen Maivelynn was a kind and gracious queen. She listened to her council, even when Allie could tell Maivelynn found their concerns irrelevant as when Lady Marissa had been shocked by Allie's lack of knowledge. Even when she was firm, Maivelynn showed care and respect for those under her rule. Why would anyone want to hurt someone who was as kind as she was lovely?

Minutes passed without any sign of Dez, Cynthia, or

Artemios. Her muscles cramping from the small space and her quick escape, Allie wondered if she dared leave. She once again tried to focus her hearing outside the tree. Nothing. Not even a footstep. But as tempting as it was to push open the trunk and step out, even if only for a few moments to stretch, Artemios' warning echoed in her ears and so she remained where she was. "Come on, Dez," she whispered. "Hurry up!"

She dozed off for a while as time continued to crawl past. The sound of someone knocking on the tree startled her awake. "Allie? Allie, you can come out now."

"Dez?" she murmured.

"We're waiting for you, Allie. The coast is clear. Come on out."

Though Artemios had told her not to open the tree herself, Allie was so glad to hear Dez's voice she quickly pushed against the trunk with a smile. She stepped out and the tree trunk closed behind her. It took a moment for her eyes to adjust to the mid-afternoon light. A figure stood with their back to her. "Dez, what happened?"

The figure turned and instead of being greeted by her guardian, Lady Xylia stood before her smirking. "Well, that was easier than I would have thought possible. Shall we go pay the queen a visit, Allie?"

Chapter 34

Allie stared at her. "You don't seriously think I'm..."

Xylia snapped her fingers and ropes entwined about Allie's body. "Actually, I do think you're going to come. Would have been easier if you had just walked yourself, but I'm flexible." Allie opened her mouth to scream, but another snap of Xylia's fingers put a gag in her mouth. "I don't think we need to draw unnecessary attention to ourselves, do we?" Then with a laugh, she turned and began walking away with Allie floating along behind her.

Glaring at Xylia's back, Allie struggled against the bonds, which only became tighter. She knew there was nothing she could do to escape and Xylia had made sure her arms weren't free to be able to drop any sort of clue. Or could she? Her legs weren't bound as tightly. Maybe she could force one of her boots off. She tried to wriggle her foot free, but boots were a lot harder to remove without hands than sneakers were. As she struggled, she saw Dez and Cynthia crouching in the forest a few yards away. When Dez saw her, he immediately started to move, but Cynthia grabbed him and shook her head. Artemios was nowhere to be seen. While she was glad to see them and they appeared to be unharmed for the most part, she realized what a mistake it had been to separate. She should have stayed with them. Caspar and Eldred were merely a distraction. Perhaps the rogue witch had known about their presence in the forest all along. She might even have known that Cynthia went to eavesdrop on their plans.

Xylia paused ahead of her to open the entrance of a tunnel Allie assumed would lead them to the palace. Darkness enveloped them as the tunnel entrance closed behind them. Xylia murmured a few words and torches along the tunnel walls flickered with green flames. The strange light cast eerie shadows on the walls as they continued down the underground path. Rats and mice scurried around the edges and Allie fought back a shudder. She'd never much liked rodents. The tunnel reminded Allie of the fabled Labyrinth, long and winding with forks leading no one knew where. At times it seemed to double back on itself. She could only hope there wasn't a minotaur waiting for her at the end of it.

After what felt like hours, they arrived in a large cavern which would have made a great double for a mad scientist's lab. Strange equipment rested on long, wooden tables. Cabinets full of jars lined the walls. There were bottles of glowing liquid scattered over counter tops. In the center of the room, a fire pit glowed under a large, black cauldron.

"Now that you're not going to cause me grief," Xylia said and snapped her fingers. The ropes and gag disappeared. Allie didn't bother trying to run away. She knew there was nowhere for her to go. Instead she watched Xylia as she walked over to the cauldron and waved her arms over it. "'Double, double, toil and trouble; Fire burn and cauldron bubble,'" she quoted in a slow, menacing tone which sent goosebumps up Allie's arms even more than the drama student who'd read the lines in high school. "How little Shakespeare knew of our kind. But that's the sort of thing everyone remembers. Witches are scary, ugly," she paused and her icy gaze fell on Allie, "evil. But think of how much good we've done for the world. Did you know most of the world's cures and medicines were discovered by witches? In fact, we are often the best healers.

And, of course, our people have been leading the way to taking better care of the environment. We've taught people about sustainability, using every part you can, recycling, all those things which are creating good in this world. Even Nyx wasn't all bad, but no one remembers the good she did. Her research would have led to a world without pain or disease. A world freed from death. Doesn't that sound wonderful? To live forever in health. But people fear the unknown and the work she did was called irresponsible. Illegal! Nyx has been entirely erased from human memory and nearly erased from Fey memory."

"Witches aren't the only ones who have had prejudices against them."

Xylia laughed darkly. "Oh? I suppose Lord Nightwind tried to convince you that unicorns have had their share of bad press. Tell me, Allie, have you ever heard of an evil unicorn?" She paused only a moment before continuing, "Or perhaps you'd like to explain to me why it is that most Fey beings are given an actual distinction between dark and light. Sirens versus mermaids, imps versus fairies. Even for elves, there are dark elves and then regular elves. But witches are given no distinction. There is nothing to tell you just in name who is trying to do what's right and who's choosing darkness.

Unicorns have no distinction either, but do they really need one? They're so pure by very nature that there's never been a truly dark unicorn. Witches are a different story though. Some are as good as you could please. Others are not. But there's no way to tell just by knowing what they are. And humans think we're just warts and broomsticks, mocking us with their ridiculous holidays and appalling literature. They have no idea what we're really like."

"And is this going to correct this perceived injustice?" Allie asked. "Is taking over the Fey Realm by force really going to give you what you want?"

"Of course it will," Xylia replied with a wicked smile. "You see, you've only uncovered half the plot. The rest of the plan is so much more delicious."

Allie heard footsteps in the tunnel. Hoping it was Dez and Cynthia, she tried to keep Xylia's attention. "Why don't you tell me about it?"

Laughing again, Xylia shook her head. "I'm not that stupid, princess. Unlike the villains you've seen in movies, I have no intention of sharing my devious plan with you. And before you get too excited about those footsteps behind you, those would be my helpers. I imagine at this point Dezydery and Cynthia are lying dead in the forest with your little pigeon."

"Artemios is not a pigeon," Allie snapped. "He's a hercinia."

"Whatever," Xylia sneered. She looked up. "Ah, Caspar and Eldred. Good news?"

"They won't be following us," Eldred replied with a smirk.

"Excellent. Why don't you help our princess get comfortable while I finish up a few last minute details?"

"You won't get away with this," Allie spat as Caspar and Eldred took hold of her arms.

Xylia chuckled. "Oh, but I think I will."

The two men pulled Allie back into the tunnel, taking a turn at a fork she didn't remember seeing before. They stopped in front of a dingy cell and tossed her roughly inside. Eldred closed the iron gate and locked it. "That should keep you out of trouble until Lady Xylia is ready for you," Eldred said. He turned to Caspar. "You keep an eye on her. I'm going to go find some lunch."

"Remember what Xylia said, there's no room for error today," Caspar warned.

Eldred waved away his concerns. "There's no one else to come to her rescue. You want anything?"

Caspar shook his head. "No, you go ahead." As Eldred

turned out of the tiny prison, Allie glared at Caspar. "What's your problem?" he demanded.

"Oh I don't know. I've been kidnapped by a lunatic and you've betrayed your people, your own brother," she snapped.

Running a hand through his hair, he replied, "I didn't know he was still alive. As far as I knew, everyone in our family was dead."

"How did you survive?" Allie asked.

Caspar shrugged, reminding Allie forcefully of Dez. "I got lucky. Lady Xylia found me and nursed me back to health. Found me a place to live and a job. She's not all bad, you know," he added.

"Right. Trying to overthrow a peaceful ruler, kidnapping princesses, plotting evil against the world. Sounds right up the alley of a law-abiding citizen," Allie retorted.

He scowled at her. "I'm serious. There is good in her. She wants things to be better for everyone."

"Then she shouldn't be doing this. Overthrowing Queen Maivelynn, killing me, this isn't going to solve any problems." When Caspar didn't respond Allie said quietly, "Please tell me Cynthia and Dez are still alive."

He shrugged.

"That's not an answer," Allie spat.

"What do you want me to tell you, princess?" he replied, looking away from her. "Eldred and I were given orders to ensure no one followed us into the cavern. That includes my self-righteous brother and the old witch."

Tears stung Allie's eyes. A rock on the cell floor caught her attention and she threw it as hard as she could at Caspar, hitting the back of his head.

"Ow!" he growled, turning back to her.

She narrowed her eyes, ignoring the tears spilling from them. "You're a monster."

Chapter 35

Allie wasn't sure how long she sat in the dank cell. From what Caspar said, it didn't sound like Dez or Cynthia would be coming to rescue her. Ever. Any ideas she had of escaping on her own were immediately rejected as she didn't have the tools to make them work.

At some point Eldred came back and Caspar left, giving Allie an odd look as he did. Eldred didn't speak to her, just watched her with that cold smirk of his. She wished she had another rock she could throw. She remembered the small stone in her pocket, but refused to take it out. She was certain if Eldred saw it, he would try to take it away from her. As much as she wanted to wipe the smirk from his face, throwing the one potential weapon she did have didn't seem like such a good idea. Shoving her hands in her pockets, she felt the stone, running her fingers over and around it, and tried to think of how she could use it. It wouldn't do anything about the cell she was locked in. It wouldn't really be all that effective at taking out her guard. Even if she had amazing aim, it wouldn't cause enough damage to allow her time to run away. Not to mention she was still locked in a prison cell.

"Hey, what do you have in your pocket?" Eldred demanded.

"Nothing," Allie fibbed. "Just my hands."

"Your hands don't glow," he sneered. "Show me what you have in your pocket."

Allie didn't have a chance to reply as Caspar walked into the area. "Lady Xylia says it's time."

"She's got some sort of magic hidden," Eldred said, pointing a long finger in Allie's direction.

Allie caught Caspar's eye and for a split moment, she saw something that reminded her of Dez. Of the goodness she saw in him. "What makes you think that?" he asked at length.

"Her pocket was glowing."

Caspar shrugged and turned back to Eldred. "Probably one of those mini-flashlights humans are so fond of."

"It didn't look like a flashlight beam," Eldred insisted.

With an exasperated sigh, Caspar said, "Look, you can take the time to search her and make us late, which would ruin everything Lady Xylia has set in motion."

"Any council meeting would do," Eldred replied.

"No, only tonight will all the minor Fey be invited to the meeting to express their concerns. Lady Xylia needs everyone present. You know this. So search the princess if you must, or you can forget about whatever she has in her pocket. Either way, it's not going to be of any use to her or you."

Eldred scowled. "I hope you're right."

"Let's just get the princess back to the palace," Caspar retorted. "Lady Xylia is already there for the final Fey Council meeting. Tonight will be a night no one in the Fey Realm will ever be able to forget."

~*~

Bound once again in ropes and gag, Allie was thrown over Eldred's shoulder like a sack of potatoes as they left the cavern and walked through a different tunnel to the palace. Allie still didn't understand fully what Lady Xylia was thinking. If she really wanted justice for her people and for changes to be made, there were surely better ways than this of getting them accomplished. What would this prove except that witches really were all the things Xylia claimed they weren't?

When they entered the palace, Allie recognized how close they were to the council room. She struggled and Eldred bounced his shoulder, causing her to hit her stomach with a muffled yelp. "Quit wiggling so much," he hissed. "Falling to the floor would be painful from that height. Especially with no way to slow your fall."

"Shush," Caspar warned. He led the way to the council room doors. Waiting and listening, he glanced down the hall to make sure there was no one nearby. "Now," he mouthed. He threw the doors open and strode into the room with Eldred behind him. In a booming voice he asked, "Perhaps, members of the Fey Council, rather than asking why someone would have kidnapped the princess, you should be asking whom."

Eldred tossed Allie to the floor and she gasped as pain shot through her arm and side from the impact. "Would you like her back?" he asked.

"Allie!" Grandma cried.

"Guardians, arrest these two!" Drake ordered, jumping from his seat.

The guardians posted along the walls of the room rushed forward. Darkness gathered around Eldred and he lifted his hands. As though blown back by a strong wind, the guardians were thrown from their feet and flung against the walls. Jackalopes, tiny sprites, and other creatures Allie couldn't name scattered from their places as the guardians continued to try unsuccessfully to reach Allie and her captors. Many of the council members began drawing on their own magic to help, but were outmatched by Eldred's powerful blasts.

Nightwind whinnied and charged, his horn crackling with power. He hit the elf in the side, causing Eldred to fly through the air and land in a heap near the council room doors. He started to charge Caspar only to be tossed back by a burst of magic from the circle of Fey Council members.

"Such violence," Xylia said calmly as everyone turned to her in shock. "I'm sure there are better ways to continue the discussion at hand. Caspar, untie the princess, if you please."

He nodded and bent down to release Allie from the ropes holding her bound. "If you value your life or the life of anyone in here," he whispered as council members began arguing, "you will sit quietly and only act when given the signal."

"Are you helping me?" Allie asked.

Caspar didn't reply, but turned his attention back to the bickering Fey Council.

Grandma pushed her way past the council members to

Allie's side. "Are you all right?"

Allie shrugged, knowing it wasn't the best answer, but honestly unsure what to say.

"Lady Xylia," Queen Maivelynn said, silencing the commotion, "I hope you are not involved in whatever is going on here."

"Me, my queen?" Xylia asked innocently. "Why would you believe any ill-doing from me?"

"I suppose you could begin by explaining why you attacked Lord Nightwind when he was clearly doing his job as a guardian and member of this council," Hazel replied, her eyes narrowed. "You could also explain how you know these villains."

Xylia smiled. "I could do that, I suppose. The answer is quite simple. Eldred and Caspar found the princess and returned her to the palace. Then without waiting to ask questions, this council demanded they be arrested."

"The elf threw our princess to the floor," Drake spat. "What were we supposed to do? Offer him a medal?"

"Oh no, I don't think that would have been the appropriate response either," Xylia said, her voice calm and even. "But didn't you even wonder why she would have been brought back at this precise moment? Don't you have questions for our heroes?"

"These are no heroes," Marissa retorted, waving a hand at Caspar and Eldred. "They bring the princess bound and gagged, then toss her before us like she was less than an animal. Lords Drake and Nightwind did exactly as they should have and you have hampered their abilities to do their jobs on the council. This is most unlike you, Lady Xylia."

"Is it really?" Xylia chuckled, her staff gathering magic to itself once again. "Are you quite sure?" She pointed her staff to the ceiling and long, glassy spikes appeared from the ground, surrounding the council members and most of the creatures within the room. The guardians and Nightwind were left outside the circle. What few weapons those within the circle had burst to shards before them. "Let it be known that this day, your entire world changes," she cried, her voice echoing through the room.

Chapter 36

The council members looked at Xylia in shock. "Lady Xylia, why?" Queen Maivelynn asked.

"Why?" she repeated. "Because the most powerful ruler we've ever had is not represented anywhere in the Fey Palace. Because the most powerful group of Fey are treated with suspicion and mistrust. Because the mortal world looks upon people like me with scorn and ridicule. I could continue on and on, Your Majesty, but the only true reason is because I can. I am a descendant of Nyx and I have studied her work." Xylia pulled a glowing jar of green liquid from her robes and the room went silent. "I have in my hands, the power of immortality. This means I have the ability to rule the Fey

Realm not just for a few years or even a few decades, but forever. There is but one ingredient left to add." She turned with a malevolent smile to Allie. "The blood of an elfin princess."

Allie felt the color drain from her face. Grandma moved in front of her as though to offer some protection. She could see Nightwind slowly rising to his feet, but he was outside the circle Xylia had created.

"Xylia, you don't have to do this," Maivelynn said quietly. "You have broken many of our laws, but we can offer you a lesser punishment if you put an end to this now."

The witch laughed, the sound echoing throughout the room. "You don't really think I'm going to fall for that do you? I will have the throne and once I have total control of the Fey Realm, I'll slowly take over the mortal sphere until everyone is under my command."

Maivelynn rose from her throne and her form shimmered as power surged through her. Bronze armor appeared over her green gown. "I will not allow you to harm the future Queen of the Fey. Allisatravondaresta Jones, Princess of the Fey is under my protection and only through my death will that protection be lifted."

Xylia smirked. "Well then, my queen, you have simply

278

added another step to the process." Magic gathered to the end of her staff, but Maivelynn wasn't waiting. A golden wand appeared in the queen's hand and she pointed it at Xylia, an arc of light shooting from it and sending the witch backwards.

The battle continued as Allie watched helplessly. Was there nothing she could do? A flash of light appeared outside the window. "Artemios?" Allie breathed. She looked closer and saw two figures crouched outside. *Is it possible?* she wondered. She glanced at Caspar who nodded. The round stone in her pocket warmed and she knew exactly what to do with it. She wrapped her hand around it and pulled it from the pocket, noticing the bluish glow surrounding it. Drawing on her power as Princess of the Fey, Allie held the rock above her head. A single, shrill note rang out and the glass windows shattered as did the spiked perimeter Xylia had created. Guardians swept in to protect the queen and Nightwind whinnied in triumph as he galloped into the fray. Dez and Cynthia ran in from outside while Artemios swooped past Xylia, talons outstretched.

"I cannot say how happy I am to see you unharmed, my princess," Artemios said as he flew past her.

"Well, mostly," Grandma muttered. "I've got to get you out of here."

"We can't leave them," Allie argued.

"But we need to," Grandma insisted. "Xylia is outnumbered and outmatched. The battle won't go on forever. And in the best interest of our people, you need to be safe."

A blast of magic swept over them, throwing people back and sending the broken glass flying. Pained cries rang out as the shards hit those without protection. Allie gasped as a jagged piece of glass ripped through her sleeve and cut her arm. Goblin-like creatures appeared out of nowhere, attacking those fighting against the witch.

Xylia took the opportunity to run to Allie's side with the potion bottle in her hand. "Once my spell is complete, there will be no stopping me," she cried as she grabbed Allie's arm. "No matter how many guardians the queen sends."

Allie bit back a scream as Xylia squeezed the wound on her arm. Blood dripped into the potion bottle. The liquid inside changed from green to red and then to brilliant white.

"At last. Immortality will be mine," Xylia said in triumph.

"Not if I can stop you." Allie tried to snatch the bottle, but Xylia raised her staff, sending her backwards.

Xylia raised the jar in a mock toast. "Nice try, princess."

As the witch lifted the bottle to her mouth, Allie felt the stone in her hand warm. Perhaps with a little luck, she could hit the bottle. She raised her arm and threw the stone, hoping her aim would be true. She watched as it hit the glass jar, just as Xylia was about to drink. The glass shattered and the potion spilled out onto the floor, soon losing its shining light.

"No!" Xylia screamed. "You will pay for this!" She raised her staff as magic gathered to it.

"Allie, watch out!" Dez shouted, running toward her. Xylia turned to aim the staff at him. A burst of light shot from it.

"Dez!" Allie cried while Caspar pushed his brother aside, the spell hitting him in the chest.

Xylia raised her staff again, but dropped it when a burst of energy hit her arm. Another flash of magic and Xylia's staff shattered, splinters of wood flying in all directions. The goblins she'd conjured disappeared as Hazel and Cynthia stood over her. They kept their staffs trained on her, magic crackling through them, as Queen Maivelynn walked to her. "Last chance, Xylia," she said in a low voice. "Give up this foolish attempt at an overthrow or suffer the consequences of your treason."

"I will never stop trying to take what is rightfully mine," Xylia spat. "You may have won today, but this is only the beginning."

A deep sense of sorrow emanated from Maivelynn as she

replied, "So be it." She pointed her wand at Xylia's chest and a red streak of light flew from it. Xylia slumped to the ground as Maivelynn turned away, a tear coursing down her cheek. Two guardians came forward and picked up the body. "Please take care of burying her tonight," Maivelynn said.

"As you wish, Your Majesty."

Maivelynn turned to Allie. "Are you going to be all right?"

"Bruised, battered, and in desperate need of a long bath and maybe a vacation," Allie added with a slight smile, "but otherwise I'll be okay."

Nodding, Maivelynn continued through the room, checking on the council members and Fey creatures.

"I believe since you seem to be moving around on your own just fine," Grandma said after wrapping the cut on Allie's arm, "I'll help some of the other injured. But once we're done helping in here, you will be my only patient."

"Good plan, Grandma," Allie said. "I'm going to find Dez."

It didn't take long to find her fairy guardian. He crouched over his brother, sorrow etched on his face. He looked up at Allie, unshed tears in his eyes. "It's not fair."

She knelt next to him. If she hadn't known better, she would think Caspar merely slept. "No, it isn't. But, he led me to believe you were dead. What happened?"

"Caspar spared us," Dez said, pushing a lock of dark hair from Caspar's face. "Eldred had Cynthia and I bound to a tree and told Caspar to finish the job. Coward," Dez spat. "He left and Caspar asked how I'd survived the dragon attack. I figured there was no sense being difficult if he was going to kill me anyway, so I told him. Something changed when he heard the story. He suddenly left. Probably an hour or two later he returned and cut the ropes. He told us to wait at the castle outside the Council Room, that he would find a way to allow us in to help defeat Xylia."

"He told me to wait for his signal to act, allowing you a chance to come in," Allie recalled. "But why the change of heart?"

Dez shrugged. "I guess in part because Xylia had been lying to him. She told him the queen had left me for dead and that none of our family survived Maldran's attack. She also told him there was no way he'd be accepted into guardian training since he hadn't defeated any dark creatures. Apparently harpies don't count. That's where the scar came from. She filled him with bitterness and anger which eroded the strong sense of honor our family has always clung to." He sighed. "Before he left us, he said he hoped we would be able to rebuild our relationship."

"I suppose him saving your life was one way to do that," Allie said gently.

Nodding, Dez replied, "Yes, but now he's gone again. And this time, he's not coming back."

Chapter 37

Even with magic to help them, it took several hours to clean up the Council Room. The injured were taken either to their rooms or to guest rooms Maivelynn designated for their use. Dez and the other guardians took Caspar's body for burial. Hazel and Cynthia fixed the windows, carefully moving the glass shards while other people worked to move the chairs and thrones back to their places. Artemios checked on Allie before flying out into the night to ensure there were no other enemies coming toward the palace. "I did not like hearing the witch say this was a mere beginning," he told her.

After he reported the woods were clear, Allie insisted Artemios go rest. "It's been a busy day for you."

"And for you, my princess, but I will follow your command. Call me if you have need of me."

"I will, thank you."

When it was nearly midnight, Maivelynn insisted everyone go to their rooms for the night. "This can be finished later," she said. "For those who came to have their concerns addressed, we will reconvene after breakfast tomorrow to discuss solutions." She walked to Allie. "You and your guardian will need to be at the meeting tomorrow morning as well. We need to know everything you learned in your investigation. I can't believe after all these years of faithful service to our council, Xylia made such a horrendous decision."

"The potion she made, is it truly destroyed?" Allie asked.

Maivelynn sighed. "I don't really know, Allie. We'll have to look into that. The hardest part will be discovering her hideout. Both her henchmen are dead."

Allie looked up. "But I'm not. No one bothered to blindfold me when we were traveling. I'm fairly certain I could get back to the cavern she used."

"That's good to know." Maivelynn suppressed a yawn. "Excuse me, we should both try to sleep tonight. It won't be easy, but an attempt should be made. Good night, Allie. I'll see you in the morning."

"Good night, Queen Maivelynn." Allie replied with a small curtsy.

Maivelynn put a gentle hand on her shoulder before walking away. Allie had never seen the queen alone before, as Nightwind had already been taken to a room to recover from his injuries. Her heart broke for Maivelynn and the pain she knew the queen must be feeling. She turned and looked about. The physical damage to the room would be repaired fairly easily, but she knew it would be a long time before the emotional scars healed.

Someone took her hand and she turned to see Dez standing next to her. She leaned against his shoulder as he wrapped his arms around her. The warm, calming scent of him filled her nose and the terror of the evening slowly ebbed away. She felt his lips on her forehead and looked up at him. He kissed her gently. "I'm so glad you're safe now," he whispered, brushing her cheek.

"Me too." She winced as his hand rested on the shoulder she'd landed on when Eldred tossed her to the ground.

He frowned. "You're hurt."

"Not too badly," she hedged, attempting to shrug. Pain shot through her shoulder and she winced again.

Shaking his head, Dez muttered, "You stubborn elf. When are you going to learn to take care of yourself?"

She smirked at him. "Maybe when you do, fairy."

He chuckled. "Come on, Allie, let's find your grandmother and get you patched up."

~*~

The council meeting began in subdued tones the next morning. Queen Maivelynn paused for a moment to recognize those who had fallen during the fight, including Caspar. "While he came in on the wrong side, he proved himself loyal to the Fey Realm in the end saving the life of his brother and Gaurdian of the Fey, Dezydery Polanski. May his soul have rest."

"May his soul have rest," the others repeated.

She spoke with each of the smaller Fey representatives about the problems they were experiencing in their areas. Assigning guardians to accompany them home and investigate the issues, Maivelynn assured them their native habitats would be safe. Allie heard Dez sigh in relief as the large jackalope group bowed to the queen and followed their assigned guardians from the room. She stifled a giggle and he glared at her. When the doors shut behind the jackalopes, only the regular council members, Allie, Dez, and Cynthia were left in the room.

"Now," Maivelynn began, "we must discuss what happened yesterday and what is to be done to prevent such a thing from happening again. First though, we have a vacant seat in the council which must be filled. Cynthia Lampwick?"

Cynthia gulped and curtsied. "Yes, Your Majesty?"

Maivelynn gave one of her summery smiles. "I would like to offer you the position as a member of the Fey Council. Do you accept, Cynthia?"

She stammered, "I, I couldn't possibly, Your Majesty. I have no experience with such matters, I am old and, well..."

"You should do it, Cynthia," Allie interrupted her. "Part of what led to this problem is the prejudice, real or perceived, against descendants of Nyx and witches in general. Being one yourself, you could prove to others that loyalty to the Fey Realm is rewarded, no matter what your heritage is."

Cynthia looked at the ground. "I live in the mortal sphere. My times in the Fey Realm are brief and I prefer it that way."

"And there's no reason for you to have to change that, cousin," Hazel replied with a smile. "You have wisdom and insight which would be a valuable asset to our council."

"Really?" she asked.

"It is up to you," Maivelynn said. "However I agree with

all the points Allie and Lady Hazel have shared. The very fact that you prefer to stay in the mortal realm gives you perspective the rest of us lack."

Cynthia squared her shoulders. "Very well, my queen, I accept the position if that is where you would have me serve."

Maivelynn smiled and motioned to the empty seat in the council circle. "Welcome, Lady Cynthia, to the Fey Council."

Hesitating only for a moment, Cynthia took her place among the other Fey Council members.

A frown replaced Maivelynn's easy smile. "And now for the less pleasant task at hand. Xylia's rebellion. Her words troubled me deeply last night. Allie and Dezydery, is there anything you can tell us from your investigation which might help us make sense of this?"

Dez spoke first, telling the council the things they'd discovered as well as mentioning some of his conversation with Caspar. When he finished, Allie told them about her capture and Xylia's cryptic monologue. "It was clear she wasn't going to tell me everything, but I found it very interesting that she quoted Shakespeare's *Macbeth* as a lead-in."

"You are familiar with Shakespeare?" Maivelynn asked.

Allie nodded. "We studied his plays in high school, well a

few of them. *Macbeth* happened to be one of my favorites. In school, one of the drama students in my class was always asked to read the witches' lines after a cheerleader totally botched them. But in any case, Xylia quoted, 'Double, double, toil and trouble; fire burn and cauldron bubble,' before complaining that humans only saw witches in light of things such as what Shakespeare wrote. While she didn't come out and say it directly, I believe Xylia planned on doing much more than merely taking over the Fey Realm. I think she planned on doing something in the mortal sphere."

The council members frowned and Hazel said, "What most people do not know is that Shakespeare wrote that scene after observing a witch brewing a potion. While most of that song, as it is called, is entirely the figment of his rather vivid imagination, that couplet is a direct quote. It was often used, and still is by many witches practicing a darker side of magic, to start a potion which would bring harm to a specific person or group. Was Xylia standing over a cauldron at the time she said those words?"

"Yes, she was."

Cynthia drew in a sharp breath. "We must find that potion and destroy it."

"And we will," Maivelynn said calmly. "Thank you, Allie

and Dez, for your reports. We all have much to think about. The remaining unassigned guardians will join you in investigating Xylia's secret chamber. Cynthia can go with you to destroy the potion and ensure that any other dangerous brews are taken care of. Perhaps in searching the cavern, we can get a better idea of what Xylia was planning and make sure there aren't others in position to pick up where she left off."

Chapter 38

Getting to Xylia's hidden cavern didn't take quite as long as Allie would have expected. When they arrived, Cynthia found the cauldron and spent a few minutes observing it. "A compulsion spell," she said after a while. "There's not enough for this to have been used outside the Fey Realm, but this would have been enough to bend the Fey Council to her will."

"Why not use it yesterday then?" Allie asked.

Cynthia shook her head. "Perhaps Xylia was overly confident. She didn't foresee the united council being strong enough to resist her."

"Or, she was planning something on a larger scale," Dez said, bringing a paper over. "Look at this."

Allie took the paper from him. She recognized the water tower in town. The paper showed a diagram of the inside and how to get in. "She was planning to put this potion into the water tower. This water goes not just to the town here, but to some of the surrounding communities. I bet even diluted this potion would be enough to bend at least some of the mortals to her wishes. Right?"

"Certainly so. Mortal minds are much easier to bend than Fey," Cynthia replied. She looked again at the cauldron and took her staff from her purse. Tapping it against the side of the cauldron, she murmured a few words. The cauldron closed up around the simmering potion and shrank down until there was nothing left.

Dez dumped a nearby bucket of water on the smoldering coals. "You're sure that potion is gone?"

"Yes. No one will be able to find it now." Cynthia glanced around. "Let's gather all the papers from her work tables and take them with us. I'd rather not spend too much time down here."

Allie agreed. She and Cynthia gathered up papers while Dez instructed the other guardians to use their magic to destroy and seal the cavern once everyone was out. Once back in the palace, the three went to Hazel's chambers to go over the papers they'd found. Many were notes on various spells and potions. Cynthia and Hazel burned the papers containing notes on the immortality serum. "That in the wrong hands would be disastrous," Hazel said as the papers crumbled.

"What about the right hands?" Allie asked.

"There are no right hands. No one on this earth has the power or right to grant immortality," Cynthia replied. "That is given only to our Maker."

They continued going through the stacks of papers until they had read each one. "From all appearances, Xylia was working alone with a few connections to people in the dark parts of the realm," Hazel said, sitting back in her chair with a sigh. "I haven't seen anything which names a single co-conspirator."

"Me neither," Allie said.

"Well then, I'd say our investigation is complete," Cynthia replied. "We'll give our report to the queen and put this whole unpleasantness behind us."

"School is going to seem so tame compared to the last few days," Allie admitted.

Hazel smiled at her. "Well, you could always choose to stay here."

Allie laughed. "I don't think I could handle the excitement.

Besides, my education is important to me. While I plan to visit often, I need to continue my life in the mortal sphere. It would look strange if I just disappeared."

"I could fix that so no one would be any the wiser," Dez pointed out.

"No, Dez, having grown up with the world being normal, I need that back after everything that's happened."

"I understand, dear," Cynthia said, reaching over to pat Allie's hand. "I feel much the same way. Perhaps you and I can take a few drives out to the Fey Realm each month in your absolutely splendid vehicle."

Allie chuckled. "Only if you bring along molasses cookies for the trips."

"That's a deal, my dear," Cynthia replied with a wink.

"It's nearly lunchtime," Dez said, glancing at a wall clock. He stood. "We'd best let you ladies get ready. I'll ask for an audience with Queen Maivelynn to go over our findings. I don't think yet another council meeting is necessary for this."

"I agree," Allie said, also rising from her seat.

"We'll be there," Hazel promised.

Dez and Allie left the cousins in Hazel's rooms. Once in the hall, Dez took Allie's hand in his. "I'm glad this is over."

"Do you really think it is?" Allie asked.

He shrugged. "I hope so. There are still questions which haven't been fully answered. But perhaps those questions never will be. I've learned that sometimes things just end without everything being wrapped up neatly with a bow."

Allie giggled. "I supposed that's true." They stopped outside the suite she was sharing with her grandmother. She lifted up on her tiptoes and gave Dez a quick kiss. "Is it weird that I'm glad I was almost kidnapped?"

"Probably," Dez teased. "But the Fey have never been normal."

She laughed. "Even though this has been the most difficult experience of my life, it's such a relief to know about all of this. I can't imagine if I hadn't learned about the Fey Realm until it was my turn to be queen." She looked away from him while a blush stole over her cheeks. "And I can't imagine having never met you."

He tipped her chin so she was looking at him. "We would have crossed paths at some point, Allie," he said, his voice low. "I couldn't have resisted getting to know you forever."

She smiled as he leaned down to kiss her.

"All right you two, get out of an old woman's way so she can go eat," Grandma said as she opened the door.

Allie's cheeks burned as Dez took everything in stride.

"Pardon us, dear lady."

"Don't you sass me, child," Grandma warned. "Come on, there will be plenty of time for smooching later." She prodded them until they started moving. Dez moved ahead, saying he needed to check in with the other guardians to see how the cavern demolition had gone. "Just coworkers?" Grandma teased Allie once Dez was out of earshot.

"Drop it, Grandma," Allie replied.

Grandma laughed. "Fat chance, sweetie. You two make a good match. Loyal, determined, stubborn as the day is long."

Allie laughed. "Most people wouldn't consider that a compliment."

Chuckling, Grandma said, "Probably not. So, just how much of that has been going on lately."

"Ugh, Grandma!" Allie groaned. "I'm not going to give you a play-by-play of my love life, thank you very much. We've kissed a few times. Dez is a good person and I really like him, okay? Happy?"

Grandma smiled and gave Allie a hug. "Unbelievably so. He's the right one for you."

"Don't rush us, Grandma," Allie warned.

Instead of speaking, Grandma just winked as they walked into the dining hall.

Chapter 39

It was another quiet day at Silver Quill Gifts. Snow fluttered outside as Allie studied for finals. The shop was filled with the smell of pine and cloves. Christmas lights twinkled on the trees displayed throughout the shop. In the last two months Allie had made several trips to the Fey Realm, learning more about the people she would one day rule. She recalled the meeting with the queen after she and Dez had finished going through Xylia's papers with Hazel and Cynthia. As they told her what they'd found, she'd agreed with their assessment. "For all appearances," Maivelynn had said, "Xylia created this plan herself. I see no reason to believe anything different. However, I would urge all of us to exercise caution in the coming months until we are certain this rebellion has died out."

In the time following that, Allie spent many evenings at Cynthia's apartment. Together they enjoyed molasses cookies and getting to know the striped cat she'd recently "adopted." Their visits to the Fey Realm showed things moving back to normal without any signs of continued unrest. These visits also gave her opportunity to better get to know her uncle. Drake always asked her questions about her studies and how her family was doing. He surprised her whole family by showing up at her parents' house for Thanksgiving and for Allie's birthday a week later. After a while, Allie realized that maybe Drake and her father weren't all that different after all. Drake still frowned far more often than Dorian ever did, but he no longer constantly looked like he'd swallowed a sour lemon. She was beginning to realize how much she appreciated having her uncle in her life. She wished it hadn't taken so long for them to come together.

Dez visited her often as well, surprising her at her apartment in his little junker. They enjoyed nights out like a regular couple and sometimes had date night in the Fey realm, watching the sprites dance in the moonlight. She took a short break from her homework to admire the sparkling pendant he'd given her for her birthday. A heart-shaped aquamarine nestled in gold butterfly wings winked in the light. A smile lit her face.

"I know what you're thinking about," Tallia teased as she came in from the work room with a box of personalized ornaments. "Or rather, whom."

"Maybe I am," Allie retorted with a grin.

"So, how many more minutes until Christmas break for you?" Tallia asked.

Allie smirked at her employer and fairy godmother. "I'm not quite down to the minute countdown, but there are seven days and fourteen hours."

Tallia laughed. "Well, let's get these ornaments on display. Hopefully we won't have too many children this holiday season with oddly spelled names," she added with a wink.

"That would be nice," Allie said, "but I'm not going to hold my breath. There always seems to be someone." She followed Tallia to one of the Christmas trees and started hanging the silver stars on its branches. It didn't take long to empty the box, at which point Tallia brought another one out. Soon the trees were decked with stars, candy canes, angels, reindeer, and other ornaments. Allie stood back to admire their work. "This looks so magical."

"You should see the Fey palace," Tallia replied. "Christmas is like magic no matter where you go, but at the palace it takes on a whole new meaning."

"I can't wait to see it," Allie admitted.

Tallia smiled. "Well, I think I'm going to head back home for now. Do you need anything?"

"No, I don't think so," Allie said. "It's been pretty quiet today."

"Yeah, that happens when snow is flying. People tend to stay indoors. All right, I'll see you tomorrow," Tallia said as she walked out the door.

"Bye Tallia," Allie replied. She returned to her studies. Time crawled and her thoughts wandered repeatedly to Summer Wood and the Fey Palace. Where her family had always decorated for Christmas the day after Thanksgiving, a recent trip to the palace revealed no decorations up yet. Dez had told her the decorations wouldn't be put up until Christmas Eve. She was going crazy trying to imagine what the castle would like all decked out for the Yuletide season. Between Dez and Tallia giving hints, but little more, Allie was impatiently waiting for her semester to be over so she and her family could travel to Summer Wood for the holidays.

The bell above the door tinkled, scattering Allie's

thoughts. She glanced up from her textbook and recognized the same couple who had come that day in October when her whole life had changed. "Welcome to Silver Quill Gifts," she said with a smile.

"Hello," the woman said. "Do you have personalized ornaments? We always get one for Gyzyka to hang on the tree."

"We do, but I'm pretty sure I'll need to do the name engraving for you."

The woman sighed. "We're used to that. You would think more people would want their children's names to be creative instead of like everyone else's."

Allie chose not to comment on the fact that most parents probably wanted their children to still love them after they started kindergarten. Instead she said, "Why don't you pick out which ornament you want for her and then I'll engrave it for her?"

The man looked at her while his wife perused the selection of ornaments and then said, "Weren't you the worker who did the jewelry box for us?"

She forced a smile, having hoped they wouldn't have recognized her. "That was me."

"Oh my dear," the woman cried, "are you doing better

after your accident?"

Allie choked on a laugh. Did she seriously think Allie was suffering lasting damage from a simple fall two months ago? "I'm perfectly fine, thank you. Which ornament would you like?"

"I think we'll do the reindeer. Gyzyka so loves animals," she replied.

Taking the ornament from the woman, Allie said, "This won't take me very long at all. If you'd like, there's a table with books by a local author. She'll be coming for a book reading and signing in three days. Very cute children's stories and she's got the table up with books you can purchase today as well as a drawing to win a free copy of her newest book at the event. Check it out while I get this done."

"Thank you," the man said.

Allie walked to the back room and took care of the engraving. She heard the couple chatting in the shop as she worked. Once the ornament was finished, she put it in a box and brought it out to the shop. "Here we are."

"This is so lovely, thank you," the woman squealed.

"You're quite welcome," Allie replied with a smile. She did genuinely like making customers happy. The couple paid for the ornament and one of the books from the table Allie had shown them. "Have a great day."

"You too," the man said as he and his wife walked to the door.

The bell tinkled and someone held the door for them as they left. A wide smile spread over her face as Dez walked into the shop, shaking snowflakes from his hair. "Good afternoon, beautiful. Is it quitting time yet?" he asked, leaning over the counter to kiss Allie's cheek.

"'Fraid not," she replied.

"Pity, because I've got some news for you."

Allie leaned forward. "Oh really?"

Dez smiled, his honey eyes glowing. "Are you ready for a new adventure, Allisatravondarestra Jones?"

She returned his smile, not minding at all that he'd just used her full name. "Always."

Acknowledgements

Every story starts out in a different way. Sometimes it's an event or one of those serendipitous moments you capture something worthy of your story-telling. And sometimes it's as simple as a friend giving you a semi-snarky answer to a writing question. The question had to do with my Christmas novella, *Holly and Mr. Ivy*, and whether or not I should use the character's nicknames in the narration of the story, or only in dialogue. I got a variety of answers, but most agreed that the full name would work best for the narration if that's what they normally went by. Author friend, H. L. Burke added the codicil, "Unless the character's name is something ridiculous like Allisatravondarestra. Then just stick with the nickname."

I laughed. Oh, how I laughed and jokingly said I was going to find a way to use that name. I then discovered that my writing program has a name generator which popped up with Dezydery Polanski. Suddenly I had the beginnings of a story called *Toil and Trouble* and I bet you've guessed who the protagonists would be. So, as promised, a big thank you and ultimate creative name kudos to H. L. Burke for giving Allie that whopper of a name. (By the way, if you enjoy fantasy, superhero, or steampunk, definitely go check out her books. She is an amazing author!)

This book took me longer than expected to write. In part because it went from being a short story I would hang onto for a future anthology or just as a freebie to my amazing readers, to being a full-length novel. I could not have done this without the support of my amazing Prince Charming and my fabulous children. I so appreciate all the help you give me as I chase this writing dream, whether it's listening to me read something aloud because I'm not quite sure I like it (or I absolutely love it and you have to hear it RIGHT NOW) or doing the dishes so I have one less chore to worry about neglecting. Having you so excited to hear the next part of my stories just makes my author heart sing! Thank you for being wonderful supporters and cheerleaders.

I also wish to thank Chrissy Hehr and Julie Wilford for being my beta readers for this project. Your insight and suggestions helped make *Toil and Trouble* so much better. So thank you, ladies, for your time and your typo-catching eyes.

Finally, a great book would not be complete without a great cover. A big hug and thank you to Aaliyah Eaton for agreeing to be my cover model and to her mom, Laura, for bringing her over and letting me play paparazzi with her. I had so much fun with you ladies as we took all those pictures. The cover would not be as amazing as it is without you! Thank you!

More Books by Jaelyn Elliott

Through the Rainbow series
Into the Rainbow
A Summer of Rainbows

Standalones
Talori and the Shark (illustrated short story)
Toil and Trouble

Anthologies & Boxed Sets:
"Talori and the Shark" in Fantastic Creatures
"Leticia's Song" in Hall of Heroes

Made in the USA
Columbia, SC
14 November 2022

70891090R00188